———————————— ★ ————————————

BODIES OF EVIDENCE

"Sir." One of the young workmen spoke up. "Was this crypt ever used as a burying place? Legit, I mean. Proper funerals."

"I don't know. Why?"

The young man walked to the end of the area where they had been working. The floor was very broken, not all the old paving stones had survived the war, and of those that had, many were cracked and in pieces. One or two of the remaining stones had already been levered up.

"We had a go here first, before the foreman told us to move down the room a bit to where we found what we did. But before that I saw this—look here."

A small object could be seen through a thin veil of earth.

"Is that a finger, sir? Is that a hand?"

———————————— ★ ————————————

COFFIN IN THE MUSEUM OF CRIME

Gwendoline Butler

W❂RLDWIDE®
TORONTO • NEW YORK • LONDON
AMSTERDAM • PARIS • SYDNEY • HAMBURG
STOCKHOLM • ATHENS • TOKYO • MILAN
MADRID • WARSAW • BUDAPEST • AUCKLAND

COFFIN IN THE MUSEUM OF CRIME

A Worldwide Mystery/June 1993

First published by St. Martin's Press, Incorporated.

ISBN 0-373-26121-7

Printed in U.S.A.

AUTHOR'S NOTE

One evening in April 1988, I sat in Toynbee Hall in the East End of London, listening to Dr. David Owen give that year's Barnett Memorial Lecture. In it, he suggested the creation of a Second City of London, to be spun off from the first, to aid the economic and social regeneration of the Docklands.

The idea fascinated me, and I have made use of it to create a world for my detective, John Coffin. I hope to use it for a series of books set in this Second City.

Thank you, Dr. Owen.

On the matter of the infection that spreads through the city, I took expert advice from a virologist who does not wish to be named but whom I must thank. Any mistakes I have made are my fault and mine only.

ONE

'WHAT IS THAT CROWD?' said John Coffin, looking down from his tower at the street below. A grey London street. 'Who's dead now?'

It was a joke, but he thought a lot about death. In a way it was his job.

Death was a long-stay visitor in the district he was observing with a proprietary interest. Poverty, disease, and several wars over the centuries had seen to it. But death comes in different packets, sometimes mercifully, sometimes stealthily, sometimes brutally and murderously. The district had known plenty of that sort of death too.

In the Middle Ages an instrument of violent death, whether cudgel, knife or even a simple horse that had thrown its rider, was deemed too dangerous to be let loose on the world, was declared 'deodand', given to God.

In twentieth-century England, such an object is apt to be put by the police in a Black Museum. But perhaps the power is not thus exorcized.

'I suppose it's going a bit far to call it a crowd.' On closer inspection it appeared to be a child and two women staring at something in the gutter. But over the years John Coffin had developed a certain sensitivity to a group of people staring at something. Professional sensitivity. It usually meant trouble on the way, and that was where he came in.

He took another look down on the street at the interestingly foreshortened view of heads, one curly and golden, and two hatted in the style favoured in the district by older ladies in summer, flowered and frothy.

Yes, from up here they looked as if they were getting excited. But it was a long way down. He could ignore it.

When John Coffin, policeman, said he lived in a church, it was understandable that people looked surprised.

'St Luke's Old Church,' he would explain patiently. It was now a secular building. The bishop or someone like that had come in and deconsecrated it. Once you used to have to take the roof off, but that didn't seem to be necessary now. Or was that just for castles, when an invading army swept in and ravaged the town? Slighting a castle, wasn't it called? St Luke's had come near to slighting itself.

St Luke's, an old City church, in an area not far from the Tower of London, nor far from the maze of streets where Jack the Ripper had operated, had been in a bad way, the congregation long since diminished and the roof never quite patched up from bomb damage.

Where he lived was going to be called St Luke's Mansions (although it still looked unmistakably like a church with a bell tower and a tiny paved yard), a set of luxury apartments, but until the Post Office got round to making this clear to everyone, if you wanted your letters and visitors it was best to say you lived in St Luke's. The locals knew what you meant and it was good for outsiders to get a surprise.

When his sister Letty had told him that she had bought a church, Coffin had been surprised himself.

'I've bought you a church,' she had said.

'Oh, thanks.'

'And you're going to live in it.'

'Thanks again.'

'But it's going to be a theatre.'

This time no thanks sprang to his lips. He was silenced. His sister Lætitia Bingham never failed to surprise him, she was a lady of such enterprise and style. All he could do was listen. If Letty said he was about to live in a church which would also be a theatre, then it was what would happen. She had a way of making the impossible possible.

'Specializing in Elizabethan and Jacobean drama. It'll be a very small theatre. The smallest ever, I should think.' An uncharacteristic piece of exaggeration on her part. Lætitia was a lawyer and not a girl to overstate things, but it showed how moved she was by what she had done. 'It's a listed building, so the façade will be preserved, but inside will be three apartments and, of course, the theatre and a small theatre workshop.'

'Also the smallest ever?'

Lætitia was his much younger half-sister (same mother, different father), and she had been educated partly in England and partly in America where she had married. Twice so far, but Coffin always feared thrice. Her present husband was a rich business man with 'interests', as people say, in the City of London. Letty's own earned income (she was a lawyer, specializing in international law), was not negligible.

'I feel I am investing in my inheritance.' Letty had a young daughter and this was how it was taking her.

'I am protecting a bit of England.' She had come back to England to live after a long spell living in New York. The accident of birth which had separated her from her half-brother had given her dual nationality. She had made it work for her.

'I hope England will be grateful.' England so often wasn't. And I am to be built into it like a brick. Or damn it, perhaps she's protecting me, too.

'And besides, Lizzie thinks she might like to be an actress.' Lizzie was her daughter, all of six years old, but a determined character as young girls so often are.

'So you are protecting her too?'

'A theatre in the family is a start.'

'And who is going to manage this theatre until Lizzie is old enough to take it on?' For a moment he had a serious worry that Letty might have cast him for this part also.

'I shall get a professional, of course,' she said loftily. 'There are plenty.'

The district had once been slummy, a fine place for murder, but was becoming smarter and more fashionable by the day, as the old houses were restored by prudent City gentlemen with an eye on property values. It was so close to the financial heartlands. You could walk to the Bank of England and the Mansion House if your Porsche was in trouble, and you had the energy. Or jog or cycle, that was even smarter.

Coffin moved in as soon as his apartment was ready, even before the plaster was dry, he was desperate for somewhere to live close to his new department. As Letty had known. Cunning creature, he thought, used to being manipulated by her and by his niece.

There were to be three apartments. One in the church tower, one in the old vestry, and a third in a side chapel dedicated to St Jude, the patron saint of lost causes. The rest of the church would be turned into the theatre. All the apartments were small but luxurious and on one floor, with the exception of Coffin's which was on three. He had the tower to himself. Of the other two flats one was complete but empty, and the third still finishing.

The theatre was as yet still a plan on the architect's drawing-board, but the Theatre Workshop, which was an easier project since it was in the former Church Hall, donated by parishioners in the year of the Great Exhibition of 1851, was about to light up. John Coffin was beginning to know the faces of the actors. The woman producer he already knew, had known her for years, but at the moment the game she was playing was not to know him. Stella Pinero, a talented and ambitious actress. This was her first effort at producing.

He was a tall, slender man with broad shoulders and more muscle than appeared. Bright blue eyes, a lightly tanned skin and a neatly greying head of hair, made him better-looking now than he had been in youth. Attractive he had always been.

He was aware that he was thinner than he had been, thinner than he should be perhaps. He had been slow to recover from a stab wound accompanied by great loss of blood, the culmination of an earlier case. He was finding too that promotion, success, could be as gruelling as failure and as time-consuming.

He had changed home several times in the last decade; he hoped this was the last move. He liked where he was now, about the best place he had ever had, greatly to his taste. Letty had done him a good turn. From his top window he could see the Tower of London, the glint of sun on the dome of St Paul's, and smell the River Thames when the wind was right. He liked to be near the river, it seemed his natural companion.

He had recently received great promotion. The Development Board had created a new force to police the newly revived area of Dockhands, Thameswater, known as the Second City. His Force was independent of the Met and the City of London police. He was its Head. A reward for good work in a difficult South London district.

He took another look out of the window. What was going on down there in the street? The window was narrow, so he had to incline his head at an angle to see. The group had swelled by one member who looked like a street cleaner. He was waving his arms. Nothing to do with me, he seemed to be saying.

John Coffin turned back into his sitting-room. He chose to have his main living-room up here on the third floor where the light was better and he could look across the London roofs and tree-tops. He always liked to be high. Something psychological, no doubt, which he could not account for at the moment but going back into his past. Underneath him on the floor below was his kitchen and bathroom. He slept on what might be called the ground floor but it had a subterranean feel to it because of the thickness of the walls and the narrow windows through which not much sunlight filtered through. The local preservation society had not allowed any tinkering with the windows in the tower, but a great curve of glass by which his sitting-room was lit had been allowed on the roof behind the crenellations. Both the architect and the builder who had worked on it were local men who had known the church all their lives and respected it. Letty had chosen them with skill, knowing what she wanted and trusting them to get it for her.

When Ted Lupus, who was the builder (Edward Lupus, Builder, Pavlov Street, Leathergate, London), found his estimates had been accepted and he had a chance to meet Lætitia Bingham, he said to his wife: 'It's the chance of a lifetime, but she might be the death of me.' He had accurately assessed a certain ruthlessness in Mrs Bingham.

Inside all had been fitted out with ease and elegance by Lætitia, who demanded the highest quality in everything.

'You've got to start living up to your position,' she had said to her brother. 'No more slumming around. You are important, successful, due for a knighthood, accept it.'

He had never quite believed in his own success. It had crept up on him unannounced, unexpected. Was it enjoyable? Was it totally believable? Would it last?

But would it matter? He had kept his old friends, had built something into his life that was indestructible.

Anyway, here he was and Letty had had her way. She had employed a top interior decorator who had allowed him to keep his pictures, his books and the few handmade oriental carpets he had bought for another home in what now felt like another life. But even for these household treasures he had had to fight.

'I paid a lot of money for that one.' He had pointed to a Persian rug of delicate blues and golds.

The decorator had replied that nothing made in recent decades had real value. Only antique rugs counted.

Coffin fell back on his last defence. 'I like it.' It would be an antique one day, wouldn't it? He kept his rugs.

One of the disadvantages of climbing up the professional ladder was that he was now an organization man, running what was, in effect, a medium-sized business employing thousands of people. He was an executive and an administrator and no longer a detective.

True, his business was still crime.

In the area for which he was now Head Officer, with the provisional title of Chief Commander (a borrowing from the Met, as he was uneasily aware), the old boroughs of Spinnergate, Leathergate, Swinehouse and Easthythe joined together to form a new unit, the crimes were what they had always been through the centuries: mugging, breaking and entering, armed robbery and murder.

They did a good line in murder, showing sometimes an imaginative turn that might not have been expected of them. A Black Museum, which had resisted all attempts in the past from Met to take it over, was full of relics of their crimes in the past. Alarming relics sometimes, life had never been gentle around here.

Because it had never been a law-abiding area and nothing was going to change that, his own apartment had full electronic anti-burglar devices, but would certainly be entered one day. He had no illusions: everything could be beaten, he might be better off with a dog. But on the other hand, the church had never been vandalized and the theatre workshop seemed to be attracting local affection. His hard-bitten flock seemed proud of it.

They were even proud of having their own separate law force, rating it, so it seemed, as a mark of their achievement. They were proud of him, John Coffin. He was marked as he passed in the street on his way home, had a drink in a pub, or stopped for a newspaper.

'Can I touch you, guv, for luck?' Mimsie Marker. Mimsie had been selling newspapers on the corner by the Spinnergate Tube station for as long as anyone could remember. She wore a man's thick tweed jacket over layers of different skirts at all seasons of the year, only in summer did she vary her outfit with a flowered boater. In winter it was a man's cap. She was a well-known figure who had been photographed by a celebrated Royal photographer and appeared in *Vogue* as 'Deprived Old Age', and been on the cover of *Time* as 'a bit of Old London'. People who knew her said that so far from being deprived she kept a sock of gold in her bed with her. Krugerrands and Edward VII gold sovereigns were said to be her favoured investment.

'I love you, sir.' She peered up at him, her tanned, wrinkled but roguish face enjoying every minute of his embarrassment. He did not reply, did not believe it. 'I could really fancy you, sir.'

Her face, pressed against his arm, was younger than he had thought. Passion might still run there. He did not answer. Dignity forbade it.

'A lovely picture of you, sir, in last night's *Standard*. You in the Black Museum. You've got a boot of my grandad's in there. He was topped for killing a police constable and he left his boot behind in a sewer.'

Was she lying or telling a tale? The maddening thing was that he remembered seeing a man's boot in the glass case.

There was a problem about the Black Museum, which was why he had paid a visit. Not the sort of problem that the head of a force was usually bothered with, but there was a special reason in this case: he was an old friend of the curator. The problem was his old friend. Tom Cowley was as protective of the museum as a wild cat of her kittens and the museum as such was due to be closed down and merged with the much bigger one in the City Force. The Met and the City Force had always eyed it jealously.

Did Mimsie know all this and was this why she had mentioned the Black Museum? She was reputed to know all the gossip of the place better than anyone else. No story that passed through Mimsie's hands lost in the telling, either.

He was almost sure Mimsie was one of the women down there in the gutter. He recognized the hat. Another reason for not going down.

The telephone rang on the bracket by the fireplace. He admired his sister's architect for the skill with which a fireplace had been inserted and the interior decorator for the cunning with which she had frustrated him. It was not a real fire laid there, never would be a real fire, so in a way the architect had wasted his time, but it looked like a real fire with logs, coal and even ash which you could sprinkle down yourself as you so desired. Such luxury.

The telephone continued to ring. Since he was unlisted, only a few people had his number, none of whom he wished to speak to at the moment.

It was still early evening, he wanted a quiet night, reading, and then perhaps going out to the little Indian restaurant round the corner to eat curry. He did not really like Indian food, it gave him indigestion, but he had not yet mastered the smart microwave double oven that Letty had installed in the wall of his kitchen.

'I am easily defeated by machines,' he said to himself, with some complacency.

The telephone was still ringing. He would answer it, of course. He always did, he was constitutionally incapable of ignoring it. A mixture of curiosity and anxiety always got him to the 'phone. It was a character mix which had probably turned him into a detective in the first place. That, and the fact that at the time he simply hadn't known what else to do.

He reached out for the telephone.

'Hello, John dear.' It was his sister Letty and she only called him dear when she wanted something. For a long time he had thought himself alone in the world, give or take a wife or two, then he had discovered his half-sister Lætitia, and together they had located yet another sibling, a brother younger than both of them who lived in Scotland.

'Letty?'

'It's about William.' William was the half-brother from Scotland, he was a Writer to the Signet in Edinburgh, with an office in George Street and house in Morningside. It was remarkable how all three of them, although otherwise dissimilar, were drawn to the law. Must be something in the blood. And since the parent they had in common was their mother, it had to be her blood. Not quite what one would have expected from that fertile, elusive lady who had disappeared from all three lives, leaving them behind like unwanted luggage.

'He wants to come and visit you.'

'Ah.' Don't agree or disagree, just hang in the air, always safer with Letty.

'Needs to, he says.'

'He's not in trouble, is he?' demanded Coffin suspiciously.

'If he was he could deal with it himself, he is a lawyer, remember. Anyway, the legal system in Scotland is different from the legal system in England. He would not come to you.'

Letty paused. 'I think it is a family matter.'

'Don't tell me that there is yet another of us. That we are four!'

'No.' Letty dismissed this idea. 'I get the impression,' she went on cautiously, 'that it is about our mother.'

'He must know as much as I do, more probably. Anyway, she's been dead for years.'

'Has she?'

'I'm not young,' parried Coffin. 'I was her eldest child. If she was alive now she'd be very old indeed.'

'Have you ever seen her grave?'

'No, she died abroad.' His aunt who had brought him up had told him so. She had told him a lot of other things too, not all of which had been true.

'Or her death certificate?'

'No.'

'Then we have to assume our mother may still be alive.'

Strange how, while energetically if spasmodically pursuing a search for his lost sister and brother, he had accepted without question his mother's death. Didn't want to think about it, probably. He still thought she must be dead, though.

'I suppose I'll have to see him then, if that's what he wants.' He hadn't taken to William on their one meeting in Scotland a few years since. Letty he loved, but not William. A prim, prissy fellow. 'He's taken his time raising the question, though.'

'We don't know what has come to light.'

Letty could be difficult too, elusive, hard to pin down in argument, of which they had plenty. She probably had the best brain of all three of them.

'I don't think William likes me very much.' For that matter, he wasn't much drawn to brother William himself.

'Oh I don't believe that's true.'

'I don't think he likes anyone very much. I think he's ashamed of having a policeman for a brother.'

'That's just his Edinburgh manner.'

'Maybe. I hope he knows what he's getting into.' He himself had been so enthusiastic about seeking out his sister once he had known she existed. He had gone to evening classes on genealogy and read books called *How to Trace Your Family Tree*. In the end, Lætitia and he had found each other almost by accident.

And then gone on to flush out William. These affairs snowballed. Once you'd started, you couldn't stop it.

'The one thing you can be sure of about an Edinburgh lawyer,' said Lætitia, 'is that they know what they are getting into.'

'I'll do what I can. When is he coming?'

'I'll be in touch,' said Lætitia.

'Letty, where is your husband?'

'In New York. He has a conference there. I might be joining him for a month or two. But of course, I don't want Lizzie to drop out of school.'

'She's only six.' He wondered, as he had often lately, if she was in the process of offloading her current husband.

'It's a bad habit to get into.' Lætitia was firm. 'Especially if the child is clever. Lizzie is outstanding.'

Naturally, thought Lizzie's uncle. Poor little beast, she hasn't got a chance. She's got to be outstanding. On the other hand, he had to admit that Lizzie did have the appearance of a child who could handle her mother.

'Oh, John, the second flat, the one beneath you, is let.'

He was instantly on the alert. This could be important news. A neighbour was an important factor in this kind of set-up.

'Yes, Stella Pinero is taking it. Lovely person, isn't she?' There was a pause. 'You like her, don't you?'

'Oh yes.' Loved her once. Forgot her. Loved her again. Forgot her. No, never forgotten.

They needn't meet much. Probably would not. And after all, it made sense for her to live on the job. He had seen her coming and going, but she had apparently not noticed him. Not that she would stay with the

Theatre Workshop for long, Stella always moved on, as who should know better than he did.

While he was thinking, Lætitia had finished talking and rung off. He had the feeling he was left alone in the room with Stella. Darling Stella.

She had put on a bit of weight lately, that was why she was pretending not to see him.

The telephone rang again. This time it was Tom Cowley, the gruff voice was unmistakable. Coffin had heard it frequently as the battle to preserve the Black Museum hotted up. For some time now, Tom, canny about publicity, had been running Open Days for local groups. School parties (if they wished to come and a surprising number did), women's associations, and other bodies like the Rotarians and the Freemasons. Not to mention the press, whom Tom provided with a good strong drink paid for by funds he seemed able to tap at will. Like a lot of old policemen, Tom usually knew where to go for money.

There was a strong, if unofficial, linking between all these groups, a kind of seepage of information. Thus the Chairwoman of the Townswomen's Guild was married to one of the local journalists, Ron Peters, a keen supporter of Tom and the Black Museum. Mrs Peters was a friend of Mrs Lupus, the deputy head of St Luke's Comprehensive, who on the advice of her friend ('It's educational in the best way, Katherine, take the kids, that's my advice'), had brought two parties to view the museum and who was married to a Rotarian who was also the builder who had constructed the flats where Coffin now lived. This couple in turn were friends of the Lord Mayor of the new Dockland City, Albert Fraser, and his young, appeal-

ingly silly wife, Agnes. And all three couples knew,
although they had never spoken to, Amelia Marr who
ran the small but discreet bawdy house in Petty Po-
land Street. Amelia had come in on her own, speaking to no one but taking it all in. Mimsie Marker, of
course, knew everyone and spoke to and of them with
freedom and as it suited her. She liked Tom Cowley.
He was a 'real man'.

'Hello, you there?' He never stood on ceremony
with his old friend, not in private, anyway. 'About
tomorrow. Now I've been thinking: two Frenchmen,
a Swede and a German, that's a bit international for
me. Do you think they speak English?'

A group of high-ranking foreign policemen were on
a visit to London and the new area of Thameswater
was on their visiting list. The Black Museum in
Thameswater was to be inspected and a buffet lunch
would be served. Not the place one might choose for
a luncheon, but the truth was that Coffin's new area
was short of buildings. Architecturally speaking, he
was living from hand to mouth. Some splendid new
buildings were going up on a cleared area of dockland but would not be complete until next year.

'Sure to,' said Coffin. He did not think that Tom
was as unsophisticated as he pretended to be, but he
had never been quite sure. It was a good act.

'Of course, I won't talk to them unless I have to.'
And possibly not even then.

'So what is it, Tom?'

'We're putting on a good spread. Drinks. They
won't go short on them.'

'I knew I could trust you there, Tom.'

'These Krauts like a drink.' He liked one himself. 'Not convenient to me as it happens. I had been going to watch the West Indians at the Oval.'

'You can go later, Tom.'

'It's a one-day match.'

'I thought you called those an abomination and a spoiler of good cricket.'

'I did, but I should still have enjoyed it,' said Tom with perverse self-satisfaction.

'Are you all right, Tom?'

'Have felt better. But I'm getting a few days' leave when this bash is over. Taking the wife to Turkey for a week.' But he had something else to say. 'If we go, that is.'

'Why not?'

'I don't like leaving this place.'

'It won't run away.' Nor get closed down while you are away. Sometimes Tom reduced you to infantile rejoinders.

'Don't like leaving it unguarded. Supposing we lost something.'

Old man Marker's boot, perhaps?

'Not likely. Besides, you've got an assistant.'

'Worse than useless, she is. Not got her mind on the job.' Tom was not an admirer of career women, especially in an outfit he regarded as peculiarly meant for men. It was like mining, wasn't it? Women just didn't have the muscle, and when there was any trouble you'd want to push them behind you, wouldn't you? 'I'm not saying we've had stuff lost so far, because we haven't, but things have got moved around, out of place. If I heard someone had been in here illegally I wouldn't be surprised.'

'Don't tell me it's haunted, Tom.'

Tom ignored this pleasantry. 'Be a crime to let this place go.' It was said without joking.

'It's not going,' said John Coffin patiently. 'Not exactly. It's going to join up with the Met museum. All the contents will be preserved and displayed in a fine set of rooms. You ought to be pleased.'

But a cosy little niche that Tom Cowley enjoyed filling would be gone. Not an ambitious man, he had finally slotted himself into just the position he enjoyed in the Black Museum, where he had ruled as undisputed king. Affable and informative to all the visitors, helpful to the young constables who came in as his assistants as part of their job experience before moving on, and a careful custodian of his exhibits. The ropes, knives, the cudgels, the assortment of guns, the very bloodstained rags of some victims were displayed by him with the reverence accorded to the remains of a Tutankhamen or a holy shroud. He had developed a manner somewhere between that of a postmaster and a librarian, with the policeman only showing when his authority was threatened. It was showing now.

'Well,' he said. No more, but Coffin knew what he meant.

Some time ago he had saved John Coffin's life by providing pints of the special type of blood Coffin had needed. Just like John Coffin, his friends said, to need blood only another copper could provide. Cowley was not a man to call in a debt but the fact was there in the background. He was owed something.

'I think the matter is settled, Tom.' The truth was that the whole building, once the main station house

for one of the largest boroughs in his new unit, the old
Leathergate, was due to be demolished to make way
for a new structure. The museum could have been
moved to new premises, but there was a strong plea for
centralization and economy.

'It's territory, John, you shouldn't give away territory. Thameswater ought to have its own museum.'

He had a point there and Coffin acknowledged it,
but he had other things to fight for; his new authority
had to establish its identity in face of rivalry, envy, and
indifference. Perhaps they should keep their own museum. Thameswater stood for the future, but it
couldn't ignore its past. A past gave you another di-
mension, a kind of legitimacy. And this area had always had a strong character, brawling, lively and
independent.

Perhaps Tom Cowley had instinctively hit upon a
truth.

'I'll see you at the reception, Tom.'

He put the telephone down, conscious that he had
not handled the conversation well, and that one more
old friend would go about saying John Coffin's
changed, promotion's done him no good. There were
a lot of other Toms in his life, men he'd started out
with, served with and now left far behind.

Promotion always did change you, there was no way
round it. You were changed, those around you
changed towards you.

His doorbell sounded. One long commanding peal.
The front door was two winding flights down; even if
you hurried it took time. The bell sounded again.

'All right, I'm coming.'

Outside was a small, sturdy boy, carrying in his arms what looked like a bronzed urn. Behind him was Mimsie, he had been right about the hat, another woman, by appearance a blood relation to Mimsie Marker, and the street sweeper, always called Alf, surname unknown. The three adults were leaving the talking to the boy.

'We brought this to you, sir.'

'You did? Why?' Coffin was on his guard, it was wiser so with lads, some of whom you could trust and some of whom you couldn't. Mimsie in the background was a kind of credential, she was far too streetwise to come near anything that might mean trouble. He thought the boy was about ten, with an alert, lively face, which might have been called cheeky once, but that expression was not so much used now. 'What is it?'

'Can I put it down, sir? It's heavy.'

'Not till you've told me what it is.'

'It's a burial urn, sir.' The boy's voice was serious. 'It's got the ashes of a dead man in it.' He did put it down, thus demonstrating an independence of spirit which Coffin was to get to know.

'Or woman,' said Mimsie from the background.

'Or woman. And we found it in the gutter. But it says St Luke's Church, so we brought it to you.'

The urn which was of a fair size, bigger than such urns usually are, was certainly made of metal even if not of bronze. It looked more like a garden urn that had been adapted for this purpose.

But on it was a printed label: Black and Binder, Funeral Parlour. On the label was a typed address: St Luke's Church.

'What was it doing in the gutter?'

'I don't know, sir, I just found it. I found it first, and then these ladies and gentlemen came along and we discussed what to do. Then we thought we'd better bring it to you.'

A corporate decision eh? 'It feels too heavy to be just ashes.' Too big, he thought.

The urn was closed by a lid with a small knob on top. Watched by the three, he tried to raise it. The lid gave easily. He lifted it up, casting aside prudence which suggested that it could be a bomb.

Then he dropped the top back quickly.

'No, not ashes,' he said.

Inside was a head. He saw the matted hair, the dull open eyes, the stained, blotched skin, and felt the whiff of decay. He could not tell if he was looking at the head of a man or a woman.

TWO

STELLA PINERO WAS downstairs in the old vestry, now converted into her smart dwelling place, but as yet bare of furniture. She heard the voices on the staircase and wondered what was going on.

'I know that voice,' she said to herself, standing in what would be her bedroom. 'Doesn't change.' Her knowledge of that voice went years back.

Stella had her own entrance on one side of a newly created lobby where John Coffin also had a front door. There was a third door already prepared for the so far unfinished third residence in the Chapel of St Jude. Stella could have waited to move into this flat, which had many attractions including a large stained glass window, but she did not feel holy enough. Also she did not believe that the stained glass would suit her complexion, yellow and blue were not her colours, not on the face, anyway.

'And I am in a hurry to get settled,' she had explained to Lætitia Bingham, whom she had known even before the start of the Theatre Workshop project but had recently got to know much better. 'But this place looks fine,' and they had settled down to discuss the details of No. 2, St Luke's Mansions. 'Who did your interior decorating? Flora Apsley? I thought I recognized her style.'

'I think she's good on city properties, gets the colours right. She's done her homework, knows the sort of person who's going to live here. I mean, it's no good putting in a huge freezer for someone who hasn't even got a window-box to grow tomatoes in and isn't going to eat at home much, anyway.' Letty had assessed what the way of life of Stella, and for that matter of her half-brother John, was going to be.

'Right,' said Stella.

'But you want a good-sized refrigerator even if it's only for the ice cubes and champagne bottles.'

Stella gave her landlady a wary look. 'I'm into still mineral water myself,' she said. She was on a diet, trying to lose the weight put on over the last eighteen months of not much work. She always gained weight when she wasn't working and lost it the moment she was acting again. Another reason for never retiring, she thought, although an ex-husband with no money and a child at boarding-school were reason enough.

'And, of course, an efficient microwave is an essential,' went on Letty. 'You know how to use one?'

'Right,' said Stella. 'I can even cook with a wooden spoon.'

The two women went to the same hairdresser in both London and New York, it made a kind of bond. In Los Angeles, where their hairdresser also had a branch, they had not as yet made contact. Letty said her husband had 'a lot of business there' but she herself went but rarely. Stella said she went there only when she was filming and she 'hadn't done a lot of that lately.'

'And the carpets and curtains suit, do they?'

'Yes, fine, to my taste, strong but neutral.' Unlike John Coffin, Stella travelled light and would be bringing no carpets with her, just her clothes, some books, a few photographs (and even of these she had had a therapeutic clear-out only the other day), and a treasured ornament or two.

'Oh look, and there's a splendid shelf in the bathroom for my Oscar.'

'Is that where you keep it?'

'Just this one. I'll have to think again for the next one.' If ever, Stella thought. Fat chance. When had she made her last film?

Their eyes had met in a glance of amused understanding; they liked each other, a friendship could be put together here of the more detached, long-range sort that women rarely manage.

'Are they really made of solid gold?'

'I don't think so. Mine isn't,' said Stella absently. 'I believe I shall be happy here.' She was due for a spell of being happy. Everyone had their turn, didn't they?

'I hope the building still in process won't disturb you too much. Don't worry about security, it's pretty good. I had special locks and bolts put in. I'll see you get your keys. We used to have a caretaker on the site, but the last one left without giving notice.'

'That's the way it goes.'

'He'd been here some time, too. I think he had a quarrel with the builders. But I'm interviewing another one. And my brother has the apartment in the tower. He's a policeman.'

'I know,' said Stella. She had seen him around, and kept her distance. 'I know him. Have done for years. On and off.'

When they had first known each other, he had loved her and she had not loved him back, or not much. When they had next got together, she had loved him more, or so she thought, and he had been more casual. Now they hardly seemed to know each other at all, and that was sad. It was not how it should have been. Somehow, somewhere, they had missed a turning they should have taken.

'He's a good bloke.'

Stella had agreed, but to herself she had added: A difficult man. Too much death hanging about him. I mean, she said to herself, what is it when you make love to someone and you smell carbolic on his hands? And you say: My God, what's that, what have you been doing? And he says: Well, just something I came close to and I thought I'd better . . . Yes, wash it off. Well, what did that do to you?

The kitchen was small but well arranged.

I might even try to cook again, thought Stella. She looked at her beautifully painted nails. The only bad thing about cooking was the washing up. Her last marriage had foundered on the piles of dirty crockery filling the sink. Marry an actor, marry a successful one, and he hasn't got time to do the dishes, either! Marry a failure, and it's beneath his dignity. Somehow they had never got round to buying a dishwasher.

She opened the refrigerator. Letty had left a bottle of champagne inside with a card that just said WELCOME. The refrigerator had a nice freezer on top but this she did not open.

What was that noise she could hear? People talking loudly and a car arriving. Louder voices now. She hoped she wasn't always going to be so aware of her neighbours.

Correction: the neighbour. The only one she had so far: John Coffin.

In the living-room with a view on to the old churchyard, now turned into a piazza and garden leading to the Theatre Workshop, she paused to realize for the first time that living so close to the job would make her vulnerable to all those members of the cast she might want to avoid. There was always someone, usually more than one, in a company who wanted to argue, complain, cry or even just talk. Her present production was blessed, if that was the word, with a young actress, Lily Goldstone, from a notable theatrical family, who had strong political views. She was always trying to buttonhole Stella.

But the evening sun rested so beautifully on the wall, filling Stella with hope. I can be happy here, she thought, and she poured herself a glass of champagne from the bottle that Letty had left her. Why not? She could go back to mineral water tomorrow.

While she sipped it she stared out of the window. From another window she could see the main road. She stared.

There was a police car, with lights flashing and a party was being loaded into it. She could see a small boy, and two women wearing flowery hats, while a fourth figure seemed to be explaining that he could not leave his cleaning cart.

Good actor, that man, I like his mime, thought Stella, watching the moving figure. I must find out what is going on.

She went into the hall, flinging open her front door with a flourish, but clutching her wine.

She walked straight into John Coffin. They stared at each other.

'What's happening?'

He did not answer at once.

'No, don't tell me. Who's dead?'

He still didn't answer.

Stella shrugged and held out her hand. 'Well. It's a way to meet.' She was half amused, half cross. It was so like their whole career together, which had stretched over many years and endured many ups and downs.

'I have seen you around. I thought you were avoiding me.'

'Yes and no.' Stella showed her glass. 'Come in and have a drink. Your sister left me a bottle of champagne in the refrigerator as a coming-in present.'

'More than she did for me.' But come to think of it, perhaps she had; he hadn't opened the refrigerator since he moved in, he must take a look.

He followed Stella into the bare living-room. At least he had carpets down and pictures on the wall, he was one step ahead of her.

'You don't mind a toothglass?' Letty's interior decorator had provided two, one each side of the basin. The basin looked like pale green marble but probably was not. 'You're in the tower, aren't you? What's it like?'

'Fine,' said Coffin, adding cautiously, 'so far.'

'And what was all that commotion about?'

'Nothing that need concern us here.'

'I hope you are right. I haven't moved into a murder den, have I? With dead bodies hidden under the floorboards?'

'Of course not.'

'So what was it?'

He remembered she never gave up. And then he thought that word would soon get around about the head. Mimsie would see to that, not to mention the road-sweeper and the boy.

'I suppose I might as well tell you, but keep quiet about it. It was a head. In an urn. And it somehow got mislaid.' He did not believe that to be true for a minute.

'And turned up where?'

'In the gutter and was brought to me here.'

'Why?'

'It seemed to be addressed to here. To the church.'

Stella drank some champagne. 'Your sister told me that no bodies had been buried here for a long while.'

'That's quite true.'

Stella poured them both some more champagne. 'Drink up, it doesn't keep. So did you recognize the face?'

He shook his head. 'No.' Hard to distinguish the features in that swollen face. He hadn't tried very hard. But no, he didn't think he knew him. Or her.

'Well, someone out there has lost a head.'

'Can we stop talking about the head?'

Stella moved a step away, placing herself with unconscious artistry in mid-scene and where the spotlight of the sun fell upon her. 'I ought to congratulate you on your big success, what you've done, where you've got to.'

'Consider it said. What about you?'

'Up and down. You know how it is in this business.'

'Letty says you are going to have a big success with your production of *Hedda Gabler*.'

'We'll have to wait and see. Letty has put in a very good actor-manager. Do you know him? Charlie Driscoll.' Coffin shook his head. 'He's formed a theatre club and got Peter Pond to find the money to put on four plays. I'm doing one of them, the Ibsen. Charlie will be Judge Brack.'

'Not acting anymore?'

'Not given it up, don't think that. I might do something with Peter later. Something modern… What will happen to the head and the little party that were carrying it away?'

'They will be taken to the local station, where the head will be deposited. Then they will give statements, after which they will be driven home. Why are you so interested?'

'I believe I know the boy. He hangs around the theatre, I think he's stage-struck.'

'How old is he?'

'Older than he looks, like all of us pro's.'

'You aren't suggesting he knows anything about the head?' It was, after all, a highly theatrical discovery.

'No, of course not. But I can't think of anyone who will get more out of it than he will.' Stella picked up the bottle. 'Let's finish the champagne.'

Theatricals have a notoriously strong tolerance for drink, and so do policemen, it goes with the job, but what with not having eaten and the closeness of Stella, John Coffin began to feel as if he was floating.

Stella started again.

'And what about the head? Where will that go?'

'An inquiry will start to establish whose head and where it came from. I expect they will begin by asking questions at the funeral parlour.'

'I don't like it. The poor chap who's lost his head! Was he dead when it was cut off?'

She had a point there.

'That will be one of the questions asked. I think it was probably cut off after death.'

Either way it was nasty.

Stella shivered. 'Well, I hope it's no one I know.'

'That's not likely, is it?'

'No, none of my friends are missing,' Stella agreed. 'But some of them would have to be gone a very long time before I noticed... And then, where is the rest of him?'

'I expect we will find him,' said Coffin. Bodies had a way of turning up.

'Supposing you found two bodies, and both were headless, how would you know to whom the head belonged?'

'Stella, how much champagne have you had?'

She put her glass down on the table. 'Far too much. Would you like to take me out to dinner? I'm interested in crime at the moment.'

'We can go to the Indian place around the corner, I suppose.'

'Oh, how keen you sound.'

'I am keen. Why are you interested in crime?'

'I'm producing *Hedda Gabler*. She was a criminal, a delinquent soul if there ever was one. I don't see her as a tragic heroine but as a criminal.

'Poor Ibsen. Well, come on, let's go and eat curry. And tomorrow, if you are still interested in crime, you can come to a reception for some foreign policemen in our Black Museum and take a look round.'

The Indian restaurant, the Empress of India, was a friendly place, quiet and dark, where Stella seemed fully as well known as John Coffin, if not better.

'We often eat here after rehearsal. This is my first play as a director, but I had a part in *Trelawney of the Wells*, which opened the Workshop.'

'What part was that?'

Stella grimaced. 'Not Trelawney. I'm a year or two too old for that, alas. No, I was Mrs Mossop. I had to pad, of course.'

'Of course,' said Coffin loyally.

'But not as much as all that,' went on the ever honest Stella. 'So I've been on a diet ever since. Not tonight, though.'

Over the curried chicken and poppadoms they gossiped about the Theatre Workshop. The boy was mentioned.

'What did you say his name was?'

'Well, we call him Little Billy. What did he tell you?'

'William Larger.'

'There you are, then.'

Not for the first time, Coffin registered the sometimes simple jokes that satisfied theatre folk.

Over a last glass of wine, Stella leaned forward. She had been making up her mind to speak and the wine helped.

'Didn't tell you quite all the truth.'

'No?'

'Someone has gone missing from my circle.'

'Who?' Coffin asked.

'A girl. One of the group at the Workshop. She just went off and never came back. She had had a quarrel with some of the cast about the costumes.' Stella leaned back and looked at him. There was a lot more to tell, but she would get it all out by degrees. 'Could the head have been hers?'

'What was she like?'

'Very young. Pretty face, blonde hair and big blue eyes. Strong-boned. Quite a big girl.'

'I don't think it was her.'

'No?'

'No. Anyway, she must have had friends and family who would be missing her.'

'I don't know.' Stella was doubtful. 'She came from New Zealand. It might be some time before they noticed.'

Coffin thought about the teeth he had seen. The teeth had looked big and old. Stained and irregular. One or two missing.

'I think it was a man,' he said. 'Probably a man.'

But you could never be sure. Teeth in a dead head always looked bigger than they were.

LITTLE BILLY FELT he was not getting the attention he deserved from his parents. His arrival home in a police car had caused some concern, but now they seemed more preoccupied with a fierce discussion about selling their time-share villa in Spain. His father had recently started his own business in Leathergate and wanted every penny, whereas his mother was thinking about her suntan.

'Let me get Rowanworks off the ground and we can afford a villa in Tuscany,' pleaded his father. 'Spain's getting too crowded now, we'd be better off making a move.'

He had judged his wife aright. Tuscany was assuredly more chic. Her opposition softened.

'I do prefer Italian fashion to Spanish,' she said, giving a considered, judicial verdict.

'There you are, then. You can shop in Rome.'

'Milan is the place.'

'You shall shop in Milan, then.'

'Or Florence,' she said musingly. 'Florence may be best after all.'

'Florence, then,' said Keith.

Little Billy managed to get his voice in. 'Mum, Dad, you aren't listening to me.'

'Don't call us that,' said his mother automatically, 'it's so vulgar.'

He ignored this. 'Mum, you don't seem interested in what I found, the head in the urn.'

'I think it's horrible. You shouldn't dwell on it any more. Put it out of your mind.' She turned back to her husband. 'All right then, sell the place in Lasada.'

'Dad, there's something I want to tell you.'

'Don't encourage him, Keith.'

'Haven't you got some lines to learn?' Keith Larger paid the fees at the well-known school for young performers attended by his son and he was a man who liked to get value for his money. The boy had talent, fine, but you had to work as well. He always had.

'Word perfect.'

'That's not enough,' said his mother. She had been a theatre child herself in her time, it was from her that Billy got the urge to perform, and she understood that there was more to knowing a part than having the words.

'I think we ought to consider buying outright this time, Debbie,' said Keith, pursuing his advantage. 'Give me a year or two and I'll be ready to buy.'

His wife considered the proposition. 'We could rent somewhere while we think about it. What about Lucca?' She had several smart friends who had bought old farmhouses near Lucca. There must be more English there now than native Italians. 'Do you think we ought to go out to Italy in the autumn and start looking around?'

They plunged into their conversation, ignoring Billy.

Through the welter of words such as Tuscany, Lucca being too popular, and Valentino being right for grand clothes but really Ferragamo was so marvellous otherwise, and of course Gucci for bags, he carried on regardless. He had often sat in on such family conversations.

Over their voices, he said loudly: 'I think I know who it was in the pot. I recognized the face.' He frowned. 'Well, not the face itself. It was the hair.'

His parents did not seem to hear.

'Not by name, maybe,' continued Billy, his voice rising above theirs, 'but seen about. Someone I'd seen.'

They took no notice. Quite possibly they did not believe him.

He settled himself into thinking about what he could do with what he regarded as his nugget of information.

THE RECEPTION IN the Black Museum for the foreign visitors was a great success and not surprisingly the star was Stella Pinero.

She arrived late, when the room was already crowded, but in time to make a splendid entrance, looking suitably elegant in black, smelling of lily of the valley. She was well received (as they say in theatrical circles) by Herr Hamburg, Dr Copenhagen, Professor Uppsala (he was a very honoured criminologist), and Monsieur Bruges, these being the labels Coffin had attached to his distinguished visitors. He had their real names on a list secreted in his hand for introduction, hardly necessary except as a politeness since they all wore labels for those who were long-sighted enough to read them.

Stella, having fascinated the visitors, turned her attention to Tom Cowley.

'Now, you're the expert!'

'Wouldn't say that.' But he looked pleased.

'It's your museum.'

'Wish it was.' He cast a look at his old friend, John Coffin.

'You've got some marvellous things here.'

Marvellous was not quite the word, Coffin thought. Stella was overdoing things a bit, as she often did in private life, while being subtle and restrained on the stage. Her natural exuberance had to burst out somewhere.

'This old boot, for instance. I mean, it's so evocative of its period, isn't it? What did it do?' The boot was mounted on a small stand enclosed in a glass case. It was unpolished with the laces undone as if just cast aside. A big foot.

'The foot inside it kicked a copper in the head so that he died. His murderer tried to throw the boots away, but was caught with one on and one off.'

'An historic boot,' said Herr Hamburg, who had taken a fancy to Stella.

Had it really belonged to the grandfather of Mimsie Marker?

'What date was this murder?'

'1922, John. Louie Fischer was the killer, one of the Swinehouse gang that were operating then. They all wiped themselves out in the end. Fischer killed PC Arnold.'

It was just possible Louie had been one of Mimsie's grandfathers, then.

'And this length of rope in the case here?' Herr Hamburg pointed to a twist of dark rope displayed in a row of objects. Next to it were several guns, and a couple of knives.

'Jim Cotton, the Leathergate strangler. He did in five people with rope like that. That length was found on him while he was attacking his last victim. She got away.'

A row of guns of various kinds were displayed next to the strangler's rope, and Tom Cowley ticked off their exploits one by one: armed robbery, a murder then suicide, a multiple murder on a housing estate. The violent deaths spanned six decades and more. There was plenty of blood behind the display in this room. That was the attraction, of course, although not one that people actually put into speech.

A group of local dignitaries arrived at this point. The new Lord Mayor apologizing for being late. He was a business man, head of a large concern with factories all over the world, but whose headquarters were in Leathergate.

He was a man who knew how to be jovial to men so much less rich and powerful than he was himself. 'Had a committee, Tom. But I've brought Katherine and Ted with me.' This was Mr and Mrs Lupus. The Lord Mayor's wife, Agnes Fraser, was a friend of Katherine Lupus. 'And this is Frank Llewellyn who works with me.' Llewellyn was a neat, quiet young man, an actuary by training and temperament. He was never bored by detail and demanded little of life in the way of excitement. He too had an office in Thameswater and had been lured into local government by the persuasions of Bert Fraser, his role model at the moment, although he had had others before and might have others afterwards.

'We've come back for a second look,' said Katherine Lupus. 'I brought a school party and didn't really get a chance for a good look round.'

'That was the day two of them were taken ill, wasn't it?'

'It was,' said Katherine Lupus with feeling. 'But it was the day they had had injections on account of a school trip to Turkey.' She looked about the room with a practised eye, saw that Agnes was doing her duty as Lord Mayor's wife by talking to the foreign visitors, and not flirting with anyone personable (usually Frank Llewellyn) as was her wont, and decided she could enjoy herself. 'Oh, Miss Pinero, I am so pleased to meet you. I have watched you act so often and admired you so much.'

'Thank you.'

'You're doing Ibsen, aren't you? *Hedda Gabler?*'

'I am directing, not acting,' said Stella with a serious face. She knew exactly how to present herself to her women admirers. 'My first attempt, so I am nervous.'

'After Ibsen, you must try Strindberg,' said Professor Uppsala, promoting his own national deity. 'He is more full of passion.'

Agnes Fraser joined them. 'I hope you will do some modern work. Say Howard Brenton.' Used to exercising social glitter herself, she recognized Stella as a rival attraction. A tall, slender, girl with red-gold hair, she knew that she was younger than Stella and her jewellery was better, but Stella had what used to be called star quality. 'Or possibly some of the good new women writers.' She tried to think of some names and failed.

'I'll do anything anyone gives me a good part in,' said Stella gamely. 'There aren't so many for women.'

Agnes Fraser turned to John Coffin. 'I know your sister, Lætitia Bingham. We've worked together on a couple of committees. She chaired one.'

It did not surprise John that Lætitia was on several committees, nor that she had chaired one of them; she was a lady who managed things. He remembered he had not heard from brother William and wondered why not. It was a little niggle at the back of his mind, suggesting no good of itself.

'She's not here today?'

'No.'

Agnes lowered her voice 'I hear a head has been found, no body, just a head.'

'How did you hear that?'

'The son of some neighbours of ours found it.' The Frasers had a penthouse overlooking the River Thames, part of an old East Indian trade warehouse. In addition they had a country house (cottage, they called it, but it was said to be considerably more than that) in Berkshire, still not far away from the Thames, for which they seemed to have an affection and in which they certainly had a strong commercial interest. 'He told his mother that he knew who it was. He thinks she wasn't listening and didn't hear, but of course she was. She doesn't know if he's lying or not.'

'He's her child.' If she couldn't tell, who could?

'He does have a vivid imagination. But this time she doesn't think he's lying.'

'I'll see someone goes round to talk to him.' Or he might go himself. Little Billy had interested him. 'Has he told them who he thinks it is.'

Agnes shook her head. 'Someone from the theatre, they imagine. He's there so much.'

'Is that what his mother thinks?'

'It's what I think.' She was talking for herself as much as for Little Billy, Coffin realized. It was what she thought, and it worried her. 'It's sinister, that place, the old church ambience, don't you think? It's got a feel to it. My daughter used to go to Guide meetings in the hall and I always hated it. Nothing to do with the present use of it, something left over from the past.'

Then she smiled. 'Mind you, if anything could wipe out the past, then the current theatre group could. Some strong characters there. Have you met them?'

'Only Stella.'

Both of them turned towards the end of the room.

An enthralled audience had gathered around Stella, constantly replenished as those who had had their word with the lady, drifted away and others took their place. Coffin admired the expertise with which she dismissed some and hung on to those she still wanted round her. She was holding a kind of court, at the heart of which were the foreign policemen with Herr Hamburg maintaining his place with skill.

At the end of the room a long table was spread with a buffet where Tom Cowley was presiding over the wine.

By the table was a display cabinet. Some strange exhibits were laid out there. One woman's stocking, much laddered. An old raincoat, stained with mud. A dirty, crumpled square of linen. These were on one side, then to the right, as if associated with these objects but a little separate, was another stocking, just as laddered as the one on the other side, but of a paler shade and smaller foot. It had belonged to another woman. Still to the right was a bloodstained sheet of old newspaper. It looked yellowing and brittle, but on one side was a faint, bloody fingerprint.

'Don't you find an atmosphere in this place?' Coffin asked Agnes. 'Wine? Or would you prefer gin or whisky? Tom seems to have thought of everything. I think there's even some Perrier.'

'Oh, I do feel an atmosphere, but that's to be expected. It's full of a kind of visible evil. But it's been cleared up, the investigations are over.'

'Not that one,' said Tom Cowley, pointing to the display case. Ted Lupus, who had been looking at it, moved away hastily. 'That was a failure. The case was not cleared up. We never caught that one.'

'At home we have plenty of those,' said the policeman from Hamburg. 'More than we care for.' But he studied the case with interest.

'We thought we had the killer at one point. But it turned out not to be so,' said Cowley. 'I remember the case. Two young women, one after the other, raped and strangled. I should think we all remember it round here. A real nasty one.'

'A famous case?' asked the Belgian policeman.

'No, it got very little notice outside the district. But we had a special reason here. The first victim was a policewoman and the first suspect was a young copper.'

'Were these two young women the only victims?' asked Herr Hamburg.

It was a shrewd question, Coffin felt, with his own memories of the case flooding back.

'We always wondered that,' said Tom Cowley. 'Especially after the second killing. There was circumstantial evidence linking the policeman to the death of the first victim. When the second one was killed it looked as though he could have done that too. So he was arrested. And then, a bit later, this piece of newspaper was found. It should have been found before, but it wasn't. That was bad.'

'These things happen,' said Herr Hamburg.

'Yes, but you always feel they shouldn't.'

'They never should.'

'But they do. Anyway, there was blood on this paper. She'd bled a bit, that girl. And there was this fingerprint. Her blood. Not her fingerprint. Not the young copper's, either.'

'You have it all pat.'

'Fifteen years ago?' Cowley shrugged. 'I was young myself then.'

'Was the second victim also a policewoman?' asked Dr Copenhagen alertly.

'No. But that's clever of you, because she very nearly was. She'd applied to join as a graduate police officer, but was turned down because of eyesight.'

'And you never got anyone?'

Tom Cowley shook his head. 'One of our failures, an unsolved crime.'

'And no more murders?'

'None that we know of,' said Tom Cowley.

'And the young policeman?'

John Coffin and Tom Cowley looked at each other.

Coffin said: 'His wife had died while he was under suspicion. Childbirth. When he got out he hanged himself. That right, Tom?'

'Right,' said Tom Cowley heavily. He didn't look too well. He needed that holiday, Coffin thought.

It was amazing how some cases never lay down and died.

JOHN COFFIN and Stella Pinero walked home to St Luke's Mansions together. Without admitting it to each other, they were both edging towards a closer relationship.

'What about Herr Hamburg?' The chap had hung on.

'I'm meeting him tomorrow for dinner,' said Stella. 'He is interested in the theatre.'

I bet, thought Coffin. He was annoyed to find he minded.

They crossed the busy main road by Spinnergate Tube station, where Mimsie was sitting by her paper stand. She gave them an alert look. Today she was wearing a red straw boater with feathers at the back.

Coffin bought a paper. It was considered bad luck locally to pass Mimsie by without buying and he never ran unnecessary risks, tucked it under his arm, and they turned the corner into Black Archer Road.

'That's the house where Rosie Ascot had rooms.' She pointed to the second in a terrace of tall, yellow brick houses, some of which were due for renovation and some of which had already experienced a sharp rise in status. The house Stella indicated was still awaiting change.

'Rosie who?' said Coffin absently.

'The girl who went away.'

'Oh yes. What about her landlady? Wasn't she worried?'

'Not that sort of place. Almost a squat. No one cared.'

'What was she like, this girl? Describe her to me.'

'Tall, fair. But I can do better than that.'

Once at St Luke's Mansions, Stella led him inside her flat where packing cases stood about in the hall. 'I'm camping out. Wait a sec while I look in this box.' She rummaged in a cardboard carton, emerging with a clutch of photographs. She handed one to Coffin and dropped two on the floor.

'This her?' He was studying a publicity photograph of a smiling, blonde girl with curly hair and neat features.

'Yes, she sent in photographs when I was auditioning people for Hedda.' Stella studied the photograph.

'I didn't want her for that, I've got Goldstone, but I gave her Mrs Elvsted. She had the right look somehow. Bridie Peel has the part now.'

Coffin: 'What's this, though?' The girl was in uniform, grinning at the camera from a car. 'Don't say she was in the police force?'

'No, her agent sent that in. She had a part in a TV police series.'

'Right.' He returned the photograph. 'Hang on to that. Thanks for showing me. You staying here now?'

'As from tomorrow. But just now I am going over to the Workshop for a run through.'

Together they left Stella's flat.

The door to the main church stood open.

'Let's take a look,' said Coffin. He pushed the door further open. 'Smells a bit.'

Stella wrinkled her nose. 'Earthy. And damp.'

'Coming from the crypt. The builder has started work, digging up the floor.' He took a step forward. 'Does it seem sinister in here to you? Any bad feel?'

Stella shook her head. 'Only the smell.'

It was quite strong, an earthy decaying smell.

Stella kissed his cheek and walked on to the Theatre Workshop where a strong-minded group, such as Lily Goldstone and Charlie Driscoll, did not believe in any ghosts other than the one that walked on Friday, and the one that hung over the 'Scottish play' whose name one must not speak.

LATER THAT DAY, when he was at home again, he took a call from his sister Lætitia Bingham.

'I've heard from William. Have you?'

'No.'

'Oh well, you will. He's coming to London on the shuttle and wants us to meet him for lunch. He'll go back that night.'

'Really?' William had a more than usual economical turn of mind. If he was spending money it boded no good. 'Where?'

'He's leaving it to me to say. I shall say the White Tower, I like it there.'

Coffin decided not to interfere. He had an idea that William was perhaps, as they say in Scotland, the 'warmest' of the three of them. 'What's it about?'

'He says that he has been investigating the family archives and has found something we ought to see.'

'Family archives? What's he mean by that? I didn't know we had any.'

'Oh, that's just the way he talks. Whatever it is, we shall find out. Next week. Tuesday.'

No sooner had he put the telephone down than it rang again. This time it was Superintendent Paul Lane, a man he had worked with before and who had transferred to the new Force with him.

'Got a bit of news. You know that head you found?'

It was a rhetorical question which Coffin did not answer.

'It's the head of a man.'

'I thought so.' Not Rosie, then. Had he ever really thought it was?

'The funeral parlour deny that it is anything to do with them. Never saw him, don't know anything about him. The urn is not one they would ever use, probably came from a garden centre, they say. And as for the label, there are always some around in the office to put on flowers or some such. Anyone could have taken one.'

'Not much further forward, then.' He was wondering about Rosie Ascot.

Lane was triumphant. 'We are. It's been identified. A chap in the office here recognized the face.'

'I'm surprised.'

'Yes, but he saw the hair, apparently the way it grew reminded him and he thought about it, took another look and decided it was. The chap used to be the caretaker in St Luke's.' He paused. 'Where you are now.'

Letty had said that the caretaker had left. For ever, apparently.

'So that was where he went.'

'What's that?'

'Nothing. Name?'

'Peter Tiler. Usually called Pete. In his forties.'

'Any record?'

'No record.'

No help there, then. An ordinary man.

'He's been dead a bit. Could have been kept under refrigeration.

'Ah. That's the suggestion, is it? Not just your idea?'

'The pathologist thinks so. You can tell, apparently.'

Coffin had a passing thought for his own small freezer. Yes, it was just about head-sized. He hoped the late caretaker had not rested there.

'But that's not all. Underneath the head . . . I don't suppose you looked?'

'I did not.'

'There was a hand. Just one. The right one. Wacky, isn't it?'

LATER STILL THAT DAY, Stella went back to her new apartment, she was expecting to entertain a few friends and made for the refrigerator to investigate the chances of ice-cubes. She took a look in the freezing compartment.

She gave a scream at what she found there, and fainted.

THREE

COFFIN DID NOT HEAR the scream in his high tower since several doors and a winding staircase insulated him from it, but he was alerted by a hammering on his door and the pealing of the front-door bell. It was the old-fashioned kind of bell that you pulled, the architect thought it more in keeping with St Luke's Mansions than anything electric and had gone to considerable trouble to find an antique apparatus. The noise it made was a tribute to its long dead makers, and was one that Coffin was never able to ignore. Generations of servants must have hurried to answer it as he did now.

The bell rang back and forth, sounding its tocsin. It was still ringing as Coffin opened the door.

'What is it?'

He saw a small, plump man, with a rolling mop of curly fair hair. He had bright hazel eyes, very lightly outlined in pencil and with just a touch of mascara on the lashes.

'I'm Charlie Driscoll. From the Workshop. You don't know me, but I know you. Can you come? It's Stella. In her place. She's found something.'

The words were bubbling out, not easy to comprehend, but the urgency was clear.

He was still talking as Coffin followed him.

'Poor Stella, I mean, there she is, innocently looking into her freezer. She'd asked us all up to her new place for a drink. And did we need one after the disasters we've had with the set and everyone drying! So she left the door on the latch and JoJo and I marched in and there she was on the floor. Quite out, poor love, and who shall blame her.' He paused momentarily for breath. 'I feel sick myself and I assure you I gave the object the merest glance. Hardly a twinkle. Shut the door, Stella, I said, there's no need to lie staring at it. She was flat on the floor... I've left JoJo with her.'

Stella was still on the floor, but fully conscious. A tall, bustless, blonde girl was kneeling by her side, one hand firmly on Stella's chest, the other gripping her wrist. She appeared to be holding her down.

'Stay where you are, Stella, you're in shock. I advise you not to move till I've finished taking your pulse. Charlie, water, please.'

'Water nothing. Get off me, JoJo.'

'Charlie, help, please, she's struggling.'

JoJo Bell had had a long-running role in a TV medical soap as Dr Freda Berry, since when she had taken on the honorary role of medical adviser to any company she played with. Her ministrations were greatly feared. JoJo was also Equity rep to the company, usually a job hard to fill, but JoJo, who had an interfering nature, seemed to welcome it.

Coffin walked straight towards the refrigerator, leaving Stella extricating herself from JoJo's clutches. I know that woman's face, he thought, I believe she's a doctor.

The freezer door had closed itself. Coffin opened it to view what had upset Stella.

Inside was a hand, a hand severed at the wrist. A hard, muscular, slightly grubby hand. A left hand.

Next to the hand was a tuft of greying hair and two teeth.

Coffin closed the door hastily.

It looked as though he knew now where the head of Peter Tiler, local man, former caretaker of St Luke's, had rested.

ANYTHING INVOLVING Stella and her friends was bound to be a performance, and the drama continued in John Coffin's own towertop sitting-room.

He had led Stella there to continue her recovery while the rest of the party had trooped up behind them. Somehow, a number of the cast from the Theatre Workshop had got there too and were now sitting around, some on the floor drinking coffee, others sipping red wine. A large pot of coffee and paper mugs had arrived from somewhere... 'The deli round the corner,' he heard someone say. 'Stays open till all hours and will do anything for us. Absolutely stage-struck.' It was good coffee. Coffin patronized the delicatessen himself, but had never had room service before.

JoJo Bell, Charlie Driscoll and Lily Goldstone, these he knew, Lily by sight only but she was famous. Only here were others whom he did not know. What was he doing entertaining them?

He looked about him. There were half a dozen of the cast of the Theatre Workshop troupe arranged in various postures around the room, and someone was coming up the stairs. He opened a window so that they could all breathe.

'What about my room, my flat?' Stella was saying. She was lying back on his sofa, pillows behind her head, looking pale and lovely. It was a shock, her expression was saying, but I am being brave and fighting my emotions, this poor weak body will endure. 'I mean, will I be able to move in? Will I want to?'

'I'm afraid the police team will have to spend a few days going over it.' They were probably there now, judging from the distant but familiar noises he could hear through his open window. 'No, you can't use it just yet.'

'I don't know if I'll ever want to again!'

Charlie Driscoll had produced a bottle and some glasses. 'Have some gin, dear. I always say you can't go wrong with a gin.'

'Not neat,' said Stella. 'Put something in it.' But she reached out a hand and Charlie deposited the glass in it.

Coffin thought she was giving the performance of her life, but he wasn't sure what play it was. Not quite Shaw. Coward, could it be? Yes, more than a touch of Judith Bliss. With a slight but unconscious hint of Mrs Crummles?

'She's all shook up with what she saw,' said Charlie sympathetically.

'He might have been killed there!'

'He might have,' agreed Coffin. But he thought probably not. No sign of blood in the apartment.

'But I've given up my other place.' It was a wail of despair.

He had a bed he could give her. He thought about it. He knew from his past that he and Stella together made a combustible combination and he was a distinguished policeman now, hoping for his K. Raffish behaviour ought to be put aside. But there was something inside him that always called to people like Stella and always would.

Charlie put his arm round Stella's shoulders. 'I've got a spare room, love. You can stay there.'

Coffin subsided. Probably just as well.

'Oh, thank you, Charlie. Are you sure? Just for a couple of nights. Then I'll go back. I've decided: I'm not going to be pushed out.'

'That's my brave girl.'

'But I'll need a new refrigerator.'

Now Coffin could hear footsteps, voices and a car door opening. Strange how the noises carried on the night air. He could guess what the sounds meant. Only one query: the car would have been an ambulance and the footsteps more ponderous if what they had been carrying had been heavier.

And that was what was worrying him. Why wasn't it heavier?

A hand could be popped inside a plastic bag and placed in a box. One man could transport a hand. So that wasn't much of a problem.

But where was the rest of the body?

Some helpful soul had found his whisky bottle and was handing round nips. Strangely, all his unsought-for guests had come provided with something to drink from, mugs, glasses or plastic cups.

He was in the middle of a party, made up of the Theatre Workshop team and sundry hangers-on. He knew few of the faces: Ellie Foster, a middle-aged but still handsome character actress, whom he had seen on television; Roger Clifford, a face he did not know, but young and good-looking; Deirdre Dreamer, tiny but wild-looking, what a colour to have your hair, was it orange or yellow? That youthful couple sitting next to each other, but not looking at each other, were Bridie and Will. They didn't look happy.

They were very, very young, and seemed to him to lack something of the *brio* of the rest of his guests. Not so sure of themselves, not able to put themselves across with the same conviction.

Stella observed him and went some way to explaining.

'They're our locals.' Seeing his questioning look, she went on: 'It was part of the deal here. The Corporation gives a grant to Theatre Workshop and we employ a percentage of actors from the Drama School here. They have Equity cards and all that. They're good kids.'

'What's the matter with them?' he asked Stella, so young, so talented (or they wouldn't be in Stella's company) and in love. But obviously miserable.

'I don't know, it's worrying all of us. It's not us. We all get on beautifully, we like them and we think they like us.'

The two young people now turned towards each other, and for a moment something glowed between them and as quickly was quenched. Will moved away, Bridie started to chatter brightly, too brightly, to JoJo, who could be heard advocating the soothing powers of camomile tea.

Stella shook her head. 'It's not the way love is supposed to take you. Not at first; later, maybe. They've got the symptoms the wrong way round. Misery comes later. I suppose you think I'm being cynical?'

He shook his head. 'I was about to be even more cynical and ask if you didn't think they were making rather a meal of it?' After all, they were drama students.

'No.' Stella hesitated and seemed about to say something more. Then JoJo bore down upon her, advocating deep breathing as a cure for shock.

Someone will kill that woman one day, thought Coffin, and took a sip of his own whisky. Soon someone was going to be asking him (if they knew who he was, which he doubted) for another bottle, dear chap, and then we'll be off. Only they wouldn't be off. They'd be here till he turned them out.

Which he would be doing quite soon for Stella's sake, she still looked white.

He stood up, to find several pairs of hands reaching up to drag him down again. 'Oh, don't go yet, dear chap, the party's only just beginning. Stay a while longer.'

He had known theatricals on and off for over twenty years now, and they always took over one's life. And he had never found a way of withstanding them.

JoJo stood up, tall, firm and flat-chested. 'Sh-sh, you fool. He lives here, he's the host.'

'Oh shit,' said Lily Goldstone in a ladylike drawl. 'I'm sorry.'

He felt as if he was existing on two levels, up here all was gaiety and life, downstairs a murder investigation was starting. He was host at this party and in command of the Force dealing with the death. A man who had shut the refrigerator door, telephoned the correct desk and waited to introduce himself to the first squad car arriving before going upstairs. Stella met his eyes across the room. She got up from the couch and came across to him.

'I'll get rid of this lot. It's my fault they are here, I was going to have a party in my empty flat and I suppose they think this is it.'

JoJo called across the room: 'Stella dear, bed for you. Doctor knows best.' Somehow, she seemed to have control of a bottle of Chianti, this too from 'the deli round the corner', no doubt.

'It's not that they don't understand,' said Stella to John Coffin. 'They do, but it's their way of shutting out death. They're a bit high tonight, anyway, because we had the usual lousy rehearsal. Hence my idea of a party. Strengthening morale, you know.'

'I understand.'

'You don't really. You can't, unless you know what it's like to be in the profession. It's like being in an army always under attack. You hang together for support.'

'Police work is not unlike that.' He sounded rueful.

The front-door bell tolled its mournful peal. In period for the church it might be, but he was not going to be able to live with it.

No need to open his door, because not one of his guests belonged to a breed that closed doors behind them.

Detective-Inspector Young, his Sergeant and a uniformed officer came in together. When calling on such as John Coffin, you came in strength; protocol and good sense demanded it. He was said to be an easy man to work with but no one ventured on disrespect.

'We came straight up, sir, seeing the door was open.'

All three of them were observing with quiet interest the party taking place.

'Quite right, Inspector.'

'We've done for now. Gone over the place, re-moved the fridge and the remains. I'm afraid we'll need the place to ourselves for a few more days.'

Coffin nodded. 'Of course. That's understood.'

'And tomorrow we'd like a statement from Miss Pinero.' Not to mention one from you too, sir, he added to himself. He contented himself with smiling at Stella, whom he knew by sight, having sat through several of her films and watched her on television. He was not a theatregoer and thus had missed her Juliet and Amanda.

One by one the party were slowly disappearing down the stairs, murmuring their thanks to their host. They too were mindful of their manners. Also, the police were bad luck.

JoJo Bell pressed him by the hand and said: 'Take my advice and practise deep breathing. You need to relax.'

Lily Goldstone smiled and said nothing: she had learnt to measure her words. Stella was just behind her.

'You off too, Stella? No need unless you wish. You could stay.'

'No, I'll go with Charlie, he's got quite a comfort-able spare room, I've stayed in it before. He's every-one's friend in trouble, is Charlie.' She gave a thin smile. Charlie had taken her in when her husband threw her out. Or had she thrown herself out? She was never sure. Anyway, there had been a tremendous scene with suitcases on the pavement and furs flung out through a window, and a taxi-driver looking on with interest. That time she had gone back. Still, it counted for good with Charlie.

'As you wish.'

Not as I wish, she thought, I wish I could stay, I think I love you again, you clever beggar, but I do what is wise for here and now.

Later might be different.

'You have given me your hospitality, John, twice now. In your Black Museum and tonight. Because it was my party.' Her turn to sound rueful. 'Let me return your hospitality. We're having a rehearsal of all three acts of *Hedda* tomorrow evening and it ought to be worth seeing. Lily is marvellous.' She looked towards that strong-featured lady who could look beautiful beyond words and who could look plain. Tonight she looked plain. 'Say you will.'

'Tomorrow.'

Stella lingered. 'Go ahead, Charlie.'

'Right you are, love. I've got a taxi round the corner in Wenlock Street.'

When he had gone, weaving slightly, he was a famous drinker but jolly with it, Stella said: 'I've been trying to pluck up courage to ask. Do you know whose hand it was?'

'Probably.' It was almost certain, he thought, that it was a pair to the one in the urn and that both, one had to suppose, belonged to him who had owned the head.

Hesitantly Stella said: 'I did get a look at the hand ... It was not a woman's hand.'

'No.'

'So it wasn't anything to do with Rosie Ascot?'

'No.'

'And the head?'

'Provisionally, the head has been identified as a man called Peter Tiler.' He saw Stella's face whiten. 'Yes, he was caretaker at St Luke's.'

'I knew him. Not a nice man.' Slowly she said: 'I think I have something to tell you. But tomorrow, please?'

She leant forward and kissed his cheek, then turned and followed Charlie.

As she moved away, he called: 'Stella ...'

She turned. 'Trust?' she said.

It was a phrase pulled from an earlier part of their relationship when she had so often asked for trust and then so often not deserved it, but had at bottom, as he now recognized, been loyal.

IT WAS NOT A NIGHT for sleeping, after an hour of restless moving around his towered home, he went out to walk. It was something he liked to do, a new habit since his move.

His new province, in which he was responsible for keeping the Queen's Peace, stretched on both sides of the River Thames, touching Wapping and Poplar on one frontier and reaching towards Bermondsey and Rotherhithe on the other. To the west he looked towards the august presence of the City of London itself. But Leathergate, Swinehythe and Easthythe were a substantial entity in themselves.

Beyond his responsibilities lay the Surrey Docks, the Millwall Dock, and the great group of Royal Docks, famous names all, but he had in his care the Great Eastern Dock, a splendid Victorian creation. In addition, in St Saviour's Dock, he had possibly the oldest

Dock of all, tracing its history back to Norman times, perhaps even earlier; historians talked of Roman remains.

If he walked far enough to the south, he could trace out the area where the Dockland University was to be built. The Drama School, from which the Theatre Workshop had drawn two players, was to be an important constituent part. The Principal of the University had already been chosen and was known to Coffin. He was a tall, lean, eager man for whom Coffin had a lot of sympathy. He had a job likely to be as exacting as Coffin's own.

He guessed that both of them knew they were an experiment and that if the experiment failed then they were both expendable. The City of London itself had a great and ancient history. The Lord Mayor and his Aldermen could look back on a history of self-government going back to the time of the early English kings. The very name Alderman was Anglo-Saxon. But this new City of which he was a part was still in the making. It had to create for itself an identity and a tradition, which it might not succeed in doing.

The University existed at the moment more as in idea than a reality, with a skeleton staff and few buildings. To a certain extent this was true also of his own Force.

In a few years he might be out of a job. So would the principal of the University, both of them would see their institutions disappear or melted down into other institutions. Whereas the Lord Mayor would survive because he was a rich business man, who would come

out of it with a life peerage and might even prefer it
that way.

Coffin walked on. He himself lived on the south
side of the river but close to the Thames. St Luke's
Mansions was in Press Street, with its suggestion of the
eighteenth-century navy and its press gangs. They had
certainly operated around here, and perhaps many a
man had sought sanctuary in St Luke's. He walked
down into Bread Street, turned into Lighterman's
Walk, now lined by new bijou residences with carefully plain faces and luxury kitchens. He passed the
corner of Tapestry Close and entered Fleming Place.
The houses were remodelled Victorian tenements, once
slums, now full of extremely smart but tiny apartments, with no animals allowed where once cats,
mongrel dogs, rats and mice, not to mention fleas and
lice, had sported in spite of the best efforts of the then
inhabitants to keep clean. A jacuzzi to each bath here
these days, although the former flat-dwellers had
waited for the 'cheap' day at the public baths.

A police car travelling slowly down Viking Street
went even slower to get a look at this solitary walker
out late on a summer night. He was recognized, sa-
luted, and the car passed on. He knew that they had
his photograph in all stations so that he was known by
sight and marked. Security went that way these days.
His codename was WALKER, and this he knew too.

He had moved now on to a cobbled walkway facing the river. Fancy's Wharf, it was called. Fancy had
been a mid-nineteenth-century importer of furs and
skins from North America and had built this wharf to
receive his sealskins, beaver, fox furs and sables. The
big handsome warehouses that had lined the wharf,

and which Hitler's bombers had failed to do more than dent, now contained some of the most expensive dwelling places in his whole bailiwick. To live on Fancy's Wharf was to say you had arrived.

The Lord Mayor and his wife, Bert and Agnes Fraser, had one such apartment, as had Little Billy's parents, Keith and Deborah Larger.

John Coffin glanced up at the gaunt but elegant façade of the Fancy warehouse where a few lights still shone. It was the place above all he would have chosen to live if he could have afforded the price.

Behind one of those lights, Little Billy lay, reading a play, in defiance of his parents' orders demanding lights out before ten o'clock. But they were absent themselves at a party, and he was in the care of the au pair, who, as it happened, had given him his supper and quietly departed for a disco.

Little Billy was aware of this fact and had considered dressing and going out himself, but he knew from past experience that his parents could be relied on to appear and be awkward if he did anything of the sort. It was not that they planned it or had telepathy or had him bugged, it was just the way life was. Not that he had anything special to do, but there was something about the streets at night that fascinated him. He had done a little night wandering himself on occasion, and been caught at it and heavily punished by his parents. Financially punished, by a docking of his ample pocket money, the worst sort of punishment for a chap with commitments and a standard of living to maintain.

So it looked like an evening at home tonight.

Now, as he read the play, *Major Barbara*, and assigned himself the part of Andrew Undershaft, he was thinking about the head he had found. He did not, of course, know of the latest developments in the case, nor that the head had been identified by the police as that of Peter Tiler. For that matter, he had not known the man by name, but he had recognized the late caretaker of St Luke's. So he knew that much.

He thought he knew something else as well, a piece of knowledge culled from one of those night walks, not such a very late night once, but a little evening trawl through the Theatre Workshop when they had been rehearsing the play before *Hedda Gabler*. He agreed with Stella Pinero that the caretaker had not been a nice man. He had heard him whispering to Bridie and Will.

Coffin looked up at those lighted windows and walked on. He thought it might be the boy behind them, lying there, reading into the small hours. He had been a boy like that himself once. He knew he would have to talk with Little Billy.

He took a right turn towards Pavlov Street and back to St Luke's Mansions. Now he was passing the house in which Rosie Ascot had lived. Although he did not know it as yet, Bridie and Will still did live there.

At that moment, as he passed below, they were lying in the darkness on Bridie's bed. On it, not in it, and they were both fully clothed.

Bridie said: 'It was a terrible thing we did.'

Will put a hand across her mouth, silencing her. 'Don't even say it.'

Both of them were tall, blue-eyed and blessed with curly blonde hair. They looked, as someone had remarked, very much alike.

In the street below, Coffin continued his nocturnal walk. Presently he turned westwards into Pavlov Street. Here Ted Lupus had the premises for his building firm: a yard with storage sheds and offices. He was an efficient man, so that the gates into the yard were trim and neatly painted and the surrounding brick wall newly pointed.

Coffin barely glanced at it as he passed, he was feeling weary now and thinking of bed. His sitting-room still bore evidence of the party but he ignored the litter and went straight to bed.

Tired by his walk, he slept well, and awoke in a cheerful mood. After all, life was good. The day ahead would be busy, because as well as two committees which he must chair, he intended to take an active interest in the murder of Peter Tiler. If it had been murder. Even that was an assumption until they found the rest of his body.

So some questions had to be asked.

How had he died?

Why had his head been cut off and one hand deposited in the urn with the head while the other was left in a refrigerator?

Where was the rest of the body? (Although he had a notion it would soon turn up. It must.)

And who had killed him, and why?

Find the motive and the killer would emerge from the shadows. Or was that the wrong way round and the fact was that the murderer would be flushed out and then would tell them why they had done it?

He usually took his breakfast at 'the deli round the corner' where there were a few tables for those desiring coffee and a brioche. It wasn't perhaps the breakfast you expected a copper to start the day on, but these days it suited him.

Suddenly it occurred to him that the source of this new happiness was Stella. Yes, it was Stella. Not founded on a rock, then. But somehow he did not mind.

He took his usual table at the back of the shop and read the newspaper he had picked up on the way round. Come the winter, he would have to get into the way of making his own breakfast. But the truth was he enjoyed the company and friendliness of Max, the proprietor, and his plump wife and their three young daughters. The girls helped behind the counter when they were not at school.

Max gave him his coffee and a brioche and honey. 'Got some rye bread if you'd rather.'

'No, I'll stick with this.'

Max was of Czech origin but his wife was Italian, while the children were totally little Londoners. It seemed to make for a happy mix, judging by the way they joked and chattered together.

He sipped his coffee while he watched the coming and going in the shop. There was usually a flow of early customers, which Mrs Max (no one ever called her anything else as far as he knew) customarily dealt with, smiling and cheerful whatever the weather. Max seemed to be coping on his own this morning, however, although the three girls were milling around the shop, helping or hindering their father.

'More coffee?' Max wiped the table with an immaculately white cloth. He was careful about cleanliness.

Coffin held out his cup. 'And another brioche.'

'They are good this morning. Nice and fresh. I make them myself. Clara, a brioche for Mr Coffin. And pick it up with the tongs, not with your fingers, as I often tell you.'

Clara was the largest and pinkest of cheek of his children, but they were all healthy, as why should they not be, as Max had remarked only the other day, with all the immunizations and injections the school health authorities handed out.

'And was the food good?'

Coffin ceased buttering his brioche and looked up inquiringly. 'Food?'

'At the party in the Black Museum. We did the food,' Max said reproachfully. 'It came from here. It was good?'

'Excellent,' said Coffin, who had not eaten any.

Max looked proud. 'Our first big job. We have hopes of many more. The district is changing, Mr Coffin, prospering. When we first came here it was a poor district. Now rich people live here. More come every day. And they eat well. They have money to spend. They enjoy spending. There is a fine chance for a shop like mine.'

As he paid his bill, Coffin amiably agreed there was. And well deserved, he thought, as he walked to his office, Max and his wife worked hard.

He walked briskly and cheerfully. For someone who had often in the past approached his day with caution and even distrust, he now found himself looking forward to it. He was changing all right. Was it Stella? Or life itself that was causing the change?

He was sorting through his letters when his telephone rang. His secretary looked at him.

'DI Young was trying to get you. I think he has something on the Tiler case.'

News about the body was what he hoped to hear. Finding it had to come next.

'I'll take it then, Celia. Hello?'

He expected to hear Archie Young, but he knew that dark and lugubrious tone: Tom Cowley in a bad mood. 'Thought you were off on holiday, Tom.'

'Put it off for a few days.'

'You all right?' He was fond of his old friend, although sometimes groaning beneath the burden.

'Oh, nothing wrong with me. That's not it. Dr Schlauffer is ill.'

This was the policeman known to Coffin as Herr Hamburg, all top German policemen seemed to be called Doctor, he was not sure why or how. Maybe they all got honorary degrees with the rank. Dr Schlauffer was the one who had eyed Stella Pinero.

'I'm sorry. What is it?'

'Oh—' Tom was vague—'nothing much. Got a bit of a fever. Better soon, I expect, but he doesn't feel up to flying.'

Nor to going out with Stella, Coffin thought hopefully. Tom muttered something about keeping him in touch, and put the receiver down before Coffin had a chance to tell him about the other hand of Peter Tiler, for the rest of whose body they were now looking.

Coffin went back to work without thinking too much about Dr Schlauffer. But the edge of brightness had gone off his day.

The first sickening had begun.

Or at least, the first he heard of.

He looked down at his blotting-pad. Celia was scrupulous about presenting him each day with a clean surface. But he was a great doodler. He found he had drawn a man's head.

'Get Young in.' He looked at his watch. 'As soon as maybe.' Then he remembered himself at that age, always rushing, never time to eat, nearly always tired. Young had a wife who was a police officer too, as he remembered, so that made two of them. 'No, make it a couple of hours' time, and order us some coffee and sandwiches.'

FOUR

DETECTIVE-INSPECTOR YOUNG was a tall, slender man, youthful for his rank, handling himself carefully because he was talking to the man in command of the whole force but aware that he was lucky to have the chance of a direct face-to-face. He hoped his luck held.

'Superintendent Lane said I was to keep you in touch, sir.'

'I do have a personal interest,' agreed Coffin mildly. He knew what Paul Lane was up to, he was acting patron to the younger man. He had done the same himself to Paul Lane in his day. Saw he got into the right company, talked to the right people, showed his form.

You needed a patron in this business. He had had one himself in the past. A man called Charlie Dander, now dead, almost forgotten, but a good detective in his day, in a style now unpopular.

In fact, one you would not dare to follow, breaking rules, going beyond the law, flowing effortlessly into dangerous waters in pursuit of chummy, no holds barred. Probably be in prison himself now. But he had certainly made his score.

Coffin himself had always preferred a cooler way, although he would be the first to admit that he had had his wilder moments. This chap was of the new breed. Because he had cast his eye over the curriculum vitae of all the new appointments to his staff, he knew that Young had a good second-class degree from Cambridge, where he had been at Queen's College and where he had been a keen supporter of the dramatic society.

'So how's it going?'

Young hesitated. 'The hand found in the freezer by Miss Pinero—' he used the name reverently, as became one who had admired her from afar—'certainly matches the one packed in with the head. They make a pair, so the pathologists tell us.'

'And they go with the head?'

Young nodded. 'They do, sir.'

'So?'

'But we are having problems with identification.'

Coffin raised his eyebrows.

'Oh yes, sir, I know that we had a provisional identification from a man who claimed to recognize him. A chap in Superintendent Lane's office, been on the manor for years. Knew the face and the hair.' Young looked thoughtful. 'Bit of a miracle, really, he wasn't easy to know. But I'm not doubting it, either. He is Peter Tiler, all right. But we do need a next of kin identification.'

It would be nice, Coffin thought, but it was not essential. An employer would do. He wondered about Stella Pinero. She was a tough lady and could certainly stand the sight if she had to.

'Well, who is there?'

'He has a wife, sir.'

But then Young produced what was really worrying him. 'We have his address, we know where he lived. His wife still lives there.'

Coffin waited, he could see that Young was getting to it, the real problem.

'Or so we are told. The neighbours say so. But we can't seem to find his wife.'

Coffin looked at him.

'We want to go in.' Young leaned forward eagerly, he was forgetting to go slow and letting his natural exuberance show. 'I've been there myself. Looked around the house. I'm sure she's there. I just get the feel she is.'

On a side table a silver tray bore a dish of sandwiches and a pot of coffee. Coffin strolled across. 'Come and help yourself.'

Young relaxed a little, enough to take several ham sandwiches and a cup of black coffee. He looked regretfully at the cream jug but knew better than to take any. He remained standing.

'What's your wife doing now?'

'She's got six months' study leave.'

'Spending it where?'

'Back to Cambridge, sir.'

So that was where they had met. Had they made a joint decision to join the police? And what was she studying? Something feminine like child delinquents or women offenders?

No.

'She's working on urban guerrilla tactics.'

Young did not sound surprised, regretful or even proud. Just matter of fact. Obviously a thoroughly modern husband. Coffin decided he must meet WD Alice Young. Of the two of them she might be the high flyer. He liked the idea, he always liked ambitious, clever women.

'About the house,' said Coffin.

'Yes, sir?' Archie Young was instantly alert.

'I'm coming too.'

Archie Young swallowed a mouthful of hot coffee quickly. Now he knew what Superintendent Paul Lane had meant when he said: Watch for it when the Old Man bowls you a fast one.

THE QUIET ARRIVAL, the even quieter prowl round the Tiler house, the unobtrusive entry in company only with his Sergeant and possibly a WPC which Archie Young had planned, inevitably turned, now John Coffin was part of it, into more of a circus.

Three cars parked in the road, several uniformed officers, and all the neighbours watching from the window.

The sun was shining on Hillington Crescent, a cul-de-sac on the edge of a large council estate built twenty unloved years ago in an older part of his district where gentrification had not yet started. But when you said unloved, you had to recognize that here and there some people had developed an affection for their houses. In such houses, the gardens had neat hedges, tidy lawns around which roses bloomed.

But not the Tiler house. It had a patch of yellowing grass flowering with scraps of paper, empty plastic bags and the odd tin can. An elderly and cynical-looking black cat sat on the wall, observing the new arrivals with bored yellow eyes. Too wordly-wise to run away, it let them walk past with no more than a flick of its tail.

'Hello, Tiddles,' said Young, trying to make good blood, he liked cats. 'He was here before. He may be the Tilers' cat.'

'What did you do when you came before?'

'Rang the bell. Got no answer. Walked around the house. Looked in the windows. Couldn't see much. Spoke to the neighbours.'

'And what did they say?'

Young shrugged. 'Didn't say much. They hadn't seen her for some days, but they hadn't seen her go away either. Of course, they might not.'

'I shouldn't think they miss much,' said Coffin, conscious of the observation from several windows.

'Nothing crucial, no.' Young added: 'They don't know about Tiler yet, but they have heard about the head that was found in the urn, and they are getting very, very curious.'

'And Mrs. Tiler? What do they say about her?'

'That she's had mental trouble and been under treatment for it.'

Coffin considered. 'Let's take a walk around the house.'

A narrow path ran round the house to the garden behind.

'Shall I knock on the door?' queried Young.

'No, leave it. If she comes out to confront us, well and good.'

Coffin went first. He looked at the upper windows, the curtains were undrawn. There was one small window open at the side of the house. 'Seems quiet enough.'

'I just have the feeling there is someone inside,' said Young.

The garden at the back was as neglected as the front one, with overgrown grass, not deserving the name lawn, and dried-out flowerbeds. Some tenant, some time, had made a brave attempt to create a garden but it had not been kept up.

'You think she's there?'

'I just don't think this is an empty house,' said Young obstinately. 'It doesn't feel like one.'

Coffin accepted this. Policemen had such perceptions occasionally, he had had them himself, and, strangely enough, he had one now: the house was occupied.

'Let's take a walk down the garden.' He led the way forward.

'Not much to see,' said Young, but he followed.

The grass was bumpy and uncut, as if it had grown over objects left out from seasons past. A tall lilac tree bent against a side fence where a rambler rose and a honeysuckle bush struggled for life against a rampant virginia creeper. Convolvulus twined everywhere and was clearly getting the upper hand. It had nearly covered the roof of an old wooden shed at the end of the garden.

'Not much work done here lately,' said Coffin. 'I think someone had a go once, but they gave up.' He wasn't much of a gardener himself, but he had a respect for living things. A person had had one here once, but it had been some time ago.

The door of the shed stood open, had rested that way for years by the look of it. He took a look inside the shed, which was full of old jam jars and empty paint pots. A fork and a spade lay on a dirt floor. A potato had somehow managed to root itself there and was growing away vigorously, pushing upwards for the light.

Coffin closed the door. A wind had got up and the door began to bang to and fro till he put a bit of old brick against it to hold it shut. 'Let's get back to the house.'

Still no sign of life there.

'How are you getting in?'

Young produced a big bunch of keys. 'Got these from the Council Offices. They keep a set of master keys. One of these should fit.' He added, 'Didn't want to break the door down. If Mrs Tiler is in there, as I think she is, then one way and another she's in a state.'

'I think the WPC should come in with us.'

Young motioned to the girl, who came galloping over. She was a tall young woman with curly black hair and bright blue eyes.

'Yes, sir?'

'You're to come in with us. This is WPC Fisher, sir.'

'I think you'd better be the first in, Fisher,' said Coffin with a smile. 'Just in case Mrs Tiler is behind the front door listening. Go gentle. Don't want to give her too much of a shock.'

Archie Young opened the front door with his key, pushed it, then stood aside for her. The WPC went in. 'Mrs Tiler?' she said softly. The two men followed her in.

In front of them was a small hallway with three doors opening off it and a staircase rising from it. All the doors were closed.

As with all houses that have been shut up in the summer heat, there was a strong, stuffy, stale atmosphere.

There were only three of them in the hall but it felt crowded.

Young was closing the door, but Coffin stopped him. 'Leave it open.'

'The wind is strong, I'm afraid it might bang.'

'Leave it.' He raised his voice: 'Mrs Tiler, are you there?'

Silence.

'She'd come now if she was,' said the girl.

'Perhaps not. Have you ever been frightened rigid?'

She shook her head. 'I think I'd always manage to scream.'

The Inspector and John Coffin looked at each other. The house was silent, yet not empty.

One by one the ground floor doors were thrown open. An empty kitchen, tidy yet neglected at the same time, with half-washed milk bottles in the sink and a bag of litter by the back door. A white door with a latch closed what looked like a broom cupboard. A small dining-room where four chairs stood sentry-like round a polished table with an embroidered runner down the middle and a vase of artificial flowers placed dead centre. A fly buzzed in the window.

The sitting-room, which faced on to the front garden, was less tidy. Someone had been living here, drinking tea, eating biscuits and leaving crumbs and dirty cups around the room. A newspaper lay on the floor. Coffin picked it up. It was several days old.

Silently he handed it to Archie Young.

'We'd better go upstairs.'

One by one, they went through the upstairs rooms. One small room was clearly used as a dumping ground for old luggage, broken furniture and clothes that

seemed to have been worn so often they now had
bodies of their own, thickening the legs of old trousers and wrinkling the bodices of torn cotton dresses.
A second bedroom was empty except for a wardrobe
and a chest of drawers. The third bedroom had a large
bed and a dressing-table. The blankets and sheets had
been drawn up carelessly.

There was no one in the bathroom. But towels and
soap by the handbasin.

'Not here,' said Young blankly.

The house was empty but did not feel vacant.

Effie Fisher said suddenly, the words jerking out:
'That door in the kitchen, it's not a cupboard, leads to
a lobby, and then there used to be a washplace with a
boiler. I know these houses, my gran lives in one like
it. Most people turned it into a downstairs lavatory.'

The value of local knowledge, thought Coffin, you
couldn't beat it. He gave WPC Fisher a good mark.

This time it was Coffin who opened the door, which
was not even latched properly so that it swung forward at once. The inner door was not closed.

Edna Tiler hung suspended from a hook above the
lavatory, a thin cord round her neck, she was sagging
against the lavatory seat, her feet just brushing the
floor. Beyond her was a half-opened small window.

Perhaps because of the flow of air, or possibly because of the uniquely arid summer, the body was dry
and shrivelled, in a state of desiccation, almost mum-
mified, the face brown, her hair falling free.

Suddenly Effie Fisher screamed. Edna Tiler had
started to move, her feet swinging, her face turning
towards them.

'Shut the front door,' said Coffin abruptly. 'It's the through draught.' He waited in the garden while the investigating team came in to measure and photograph, and while the police surgeon undertook a first examination.

He paced slowly up and down the garden path, wishing, not for the first time, that he had not given up smoking. Across the garden fence a head appeared, then the rest of the body. A sturdy, elderly woman with her head tied in a scarf. Very few women wore scarves like that now, he thought.

'Just doing a bit of gardening,' she said. And then, more honestly: 'And watching to see what went on. I'm Mrs Armour.'

Coffin remained silent.

'She's in there, isn't she?'

'You mean Mrs Tiler?'

'Yes, I mean Mrs Tiler, as you well know. Who else? She's dead, I suppose. You needn't say. I recognized Doc Ferguson. We all know he's the police surgeon. Not the first time he's been seen round here.'

That was interesting, Coffin thought, but not surprising.

'He's gone too, hasn't he? Oh, go on, you needn't worry. Found his head in a pot, didn't you? Of course we know. You can't keep a thing like that quiet. You don't think she did it?' Mrs. Armour nodded towards the house.

Coffin remained impassive.

She peered in his face. 'Don't know you, do I? You're new here.'

Coffin nodded. 'Yes, I am.'

'What are you?'

Coffin managed an evasive answer.

She did not appreciate it. 'You're not talkative, I'll say that for you.'

'Is the black cat yours, Mrs Armour?'

'No one's cat. Not that sort. Likes his independence. I feed him, though.'

'How well did you know Mrs Tiler?'

'Not well enough. No one did. He did a power of talking when he was in the mood. Reckoned himself, he did. Especially when he got in with those theatre people.'

'Any of them ever here?' said Coffin alertly. The whole cast appeared before his mind's eye as if on a film, from Little Billy to Stella Pinero herself. JoJo Bell, Charlie Driscoll, Lily Goldstone, and that unhappy young couple, Bridie and Tom. It was hard to think of them visiting in Hillington Crescent.

'Might have been. Can't say I ever saw them,' said Mrs Armour as if she regretted the omission. 'No, they didn't have many visitors. Any visiting he did, I reckon he did elsewhere. Away from home, as you might say. Not that I would have fancied him myself.'

'I see.' He supposed she meant what he thought she did.

'Kept herself to herself, that was Edna Tiler. Nothing against that, I like to myself. But it means you can't help when help's needed.'

'And was it needed?' asked Coffin.

'A funny household,' she answered obliquely. 'I don't sleep well, so I see things others might not see. I'm a gardener too. No garden ought to look like that one.'

It was true that there was a striking difference between the neglected Tiler garden and the flowered borders next door.

'What do you mean, Mrs Armour?'

'There's a chap looking for you at the back door,' said Mrs Armour instead of answering. She disappeared behind her own hedge, bobbing away. Apparently she had been standing on something.

The police surgeon was standing at the back door, waiting for Coffin.

'Suicide,' he said. 'Probably.'

'Only probably?'

Dr Ferguson shrugged. 'You know how it is. Needs some more work.' Shortly afterwards, after satisfying himself that all was in train, John Coffin left.

At the door, he turned to Archie Young. 'Get the garden gone over,' he ordered. 'Dig it up. Spade by spade if you have to.'

As he drove away, in the garden behind him, the black cat approached the garden shed, now closed against him, and in which he had been in the habit of sleeping.

It was his territory. He was cross.

FIVE

BEHIND HIM Coffin had left a house under search and a garden about to be excavated. The days when he might have stood by and directed the investigation himself had long gone. He had been photographed by stringers for several major dailies as he left the house and that was about it. He must get back to his desk. But his strong interest remained.

As he chaired a committee, went through several significant interviews with people important to his new Force, and promised to appear on the local TV station, *London River*, to discuss peace-keeping in the district (always a thorny subject since Dickens's day and no easier to answer then than now), underneath all the time, he was thinking about the severed, the headless and so far undiscovered body, and the dead woman in Hillington Crescent.

Do names count for anything, he asked himself, and is there any significance in the way the street echoes Rillington Place of ill-fame?

Houses have histories and those histories can influence the lives of those who dwell in them, of that he was convinced, but can names affect houses?

He had a strong sense of the ramifications of the Tiler case. It was one of those cases that stretch out long fingers to touch many lives, he could feel it. Already his own had been touched by it, he was fascinated. He ought not to have been giving his mind to it, he had other responsibilities, but he found he could not stop.

There was one big question to answer first: was it suicide or murder in that house?

On the answer to that question depended others. If it was suicide, then had Mrs Tiler killed herself because she was guilty of the murder of her husband? It was a possibility that had to be considered.

The position of her body suggested she had taken her own life.

If so, and she had hanged herself because she was guilty of killing her husband, why had she done so?

Well, domestic murders were commonplace enough, and perhaps one might not have to look far for an answer. He might have beaten her, or been a drunk, or unfaithful. Or sexually exacting in a way she did not care for. Or any mixture of all these things. Coffin had enough experience to know there might never be a complete answer.

But why had she cut off his head and hands? And where was the rest of the body?

We've got to find the body, he told himself. And with a sigh, went back to his own labours. Then by way of reminding himself what his job meant and at the same time postponing the actual performance of it, he went to the office window to look out.

From this viewpoint, John Coffin could see the top of St Luke's tower on one hand and the distant spire of a Hawksmoor church on the other. This part of London had always been well provided with churches.

He wondered what the tally of historic churches was in his patch. The blitz had claimed a few, but on the whole they had survived. He had an idea they would survive the neo-paganism of the end of the twentieth century.

As well as churches, he had under his jurisdiction six hospitals, two very large and one a specialist hospital for children, founded two centuries ago and now world-famous for its operations on neonates, the newly born. In addition he had four football teams, a selection of fire-fighting forces, more schools than he could count, a polytechnic and the beginnings of a university. And, of course, several art galleries and museums, their number including the Black Museum. There was an old railway, a new railway, a network of roads, and the site for an airport where excavations had uncovered several Roman warehouses and the remains of a Neolithic hunting camp, thus holding everything up while the archaeologists got to work.

Accordingly, his authority crossed that of the DHSS, the Ministry of Education, the Ministry of the Environment, and, since there was a Naval establishment on the patch, that of the Ministry of Defence as well.

Not monarch of all he surveyed then, but just one baron among many, and by no means the most powerful.

Far below he saw an urban fox, inhabitant of the railway embankment, slide slowly out from behind a row of dustbins belonging to the Czar of Russia public house and speed with circumspect caution across the main road and into the People's Peace Park, the park named after no particular peace and no special people, just a generalized gesture of goodwill from the Depression years. The fox looked sleek, healthy and confident. By comparison, the old man sitting on the park bench looked derelict. Coffin thought about the statistics of the homeless living rough, the muggings, the rapes and the Dead on Arrival contained in files on his desk. He had them all, had all the figures.

He caught the arrogant flash of a ginger tail and he could imagine the rank emission marking the bushes. The old man got up and limped away.

It was really hard being a primate in this jungle, Coffin thought.

With new energy, he got down to his work. It was one way of fighting back. You didn't have to dig in the dustbin like that fox and send out an urgent stream to define your territory.

Not a bad idea, though, he thought.

A dozen letters dictated to Celia. Three long telephone calls to colleagues. An interview with the Bishop, who was too conservative on some issues while being too radical for the district (which returned a left-wing MP yet was essentially conservative in spirit) on others, and who alarmingly told him that he would like to have been born a woman.

The Bishop had met Lætitia, knew the Frasers, Ted and Katherine Lupus, Little Billy and his parents, and had heard about the head. On which subject he seemed to feel it necessary to make an episcopal pronouncement.

'A very strange business,' he said. 'The cutting off of the head makes a very strong statement.'

Yes, of death, thought Coffin.

But it turned out the Bishop meant pictorially. 'Have you seen the Caravaggio of the Beheading of St John the Baptist?'

'No.' Had there been any symbolism in the deliver-
ing of the head to the church? There was a St John's
Church not so far away, but the head had come to St
Luke's, so it must have been meant. Not for him personally, he hoped. There were enough queer sides to
this case as it was, without the Commander of the
Force getting a severed head as a present.

After the Bishop departed, he was on his own. The
afternoon sun came through the open window. With
it came the smell of the Thames. Centuries of being
London's workhorse had given it a smell all its own,
compounded of wet wood, coal dust and oil, and just
plain dirt. No, not compounded, a vegetable growth
of all those elements that could have been bottled. A
dark green-brown broth. It was said to be a clean river
now in which fish swam, and indeed you did see the
odd angler, although it was hard to know what fish ate
the bait, or who would choose to eat the fish that ate
it.

In stormy weather a porpoise sometimes came as far
upriver as the Tower, but Coffin did not expect to see
one himself. He was not the sort of person who saw
dolphins dancing, or porpoises playing.

The body could be in the river, of course, he had
come across bodies in the Thames before. At the beginning of his career, one terrifying murderer had used
the river as a hiding-place. But the river always delivered back its burden in the end.

He telephoned Inspector Archie Young, and being
who he was, got through to the harassed young officer at once.

'Have there been any reports of a headless body
washing up along the river or in the estuary?'

'No. I thought of that, of course, but nothing.' Young added cautiously: 'That's not to say there won't be. The river has its own way of sending bodies back. It can sometimes hang on longer than you'd think likely. And the body might have been weighted down, in which case . . .' Somehow he managed to convey a shrug across the telephone lines. 'It would turn up . . . sometime.' He didn't feel hopeful about the river, and he managed to convey this, too.

'No, I don't think Tiler's body is in the river, I agree with you,' said Coffin, answering the unspoken comment. 'What about the garden?'

'We've made a start, sir.'

'And about Mrs Tiler? Any news from the pathologist?' Murder or suicide, he meant.

'Nothing yet. I've tried to get something but he isn't giving.' To his mind that was significant in itself: the chap, usually so quick, was finding it hard to come to a conclusion. 'He might say more to you, sir.'

'Yes.'

Coffin considered telephoning the pathologist, whom he knew, a friend from the old days. He looked at the telephone. But Bill Baines was well known for resenting an interruption in the middle of his working day.

Then Celia came in with a letter. 'Delivered by hand. A boy. Got through everyone right up to here with no one stopping him!' She sounded more amused than shocked.

The letter was an elegant production in a long pale blue envelope, it was inscribed in Stella's flowing handwriting.

'*Little Billy will deliver this note. He has made himself a sort of Ganymede. Or do I mean Ariel?*' Stella had left school very young and gone straight on the stage, as Coffin knew very well, no classical education there, but the theatre had educated her. '*Anyway, he is acting messenger. He says he knows where to find you.*' Does he indeed, thought Coffin. '*This is to remind you about the rehearsal tonight. We start about six. I have invited a few other people. Don't worry about food. There will be sandwiches and coffee for all. Be punctual.*'

I'll get there if I can, he muttered. Stella had never really understood about anyone's work but her own.

AT THE THEATRE WORKSHOP, they were into what Stella called 'neurotic time': that period when the cast, their first exuberance at getting their parts at all diminished and they had had time to get nervous, begin to feel depressed, imaginative, full of small ailments and apt to quarrel. This state had not been improved by the fact that she had had to tell them earlier today that the police would be interviewing them. Perhaps she should have left it until after the rehearsal. The cast was fidgety, anyway, at having an audience, however small.

Stella had developed the habit of asking local people of standing and importance to 'drop in' to watch rehearsals. She knew the cast did not like this but she had a very good reason for it, as they had been told.

Lætitia Bingham was financing the theatre as a tax loss. Goodness knows if she was rich enough, but she seemed to think she was and Stella could only trust her. But it was a circulating trust; hardheaded Letty gave them only enough to be going on with and then they had to ask for more. She had enrolled unpaid trustees, of which the lord Mayor was, *ex officio*, one. Mrs Fraser was there on her own account, which was a cunning move on Letty's part because Agnes would stay even when her husband retired after his year of office. Ted Lupus as an important local figure was another trustee and Little Billy's mother was angling to be one.

But Letty had made it clear she expected them to raise funds for themselves. All hands to the pump, she implied. In addition, the Theatre Workshop was getting a subsidy from the Enterprise Fund. But life was expensive. They were a professional theatre, not a theatre club, and therefore had to keep the rules about fire risks. It all needed money, and about money, Letty ran a tight ship.

So Stella did her bit, and obliged the cast to do theirs, by inviting the trustees and their friends in for a look and a meeting with the cast, who were instructed to behave well.

The Lupuses were there now, they usually came together. Ted Lupus was a large, gentle man with square, workmanlike hands, whom Stella found attractive. She had been their guest at dinner, enjoying the food and admiring the terrace garden in pots. Perish the thought, Stella, she told herself, you have enough to do. Anyway, the friendliness and affection he radiated was general, he was just a man who liked women, thought they needed looking after and was willing to be the one to do it. A rich man now, he had created his business from nothing, but Kath Lupus had supported him all through the tough early days. She was both proud and protective of him. Stella offered them coffee and sandwiches, both made and delivered by Max in person (he too was a theatre buff), and thought that Kath Lupus was a lucky lady. And for such a lucky lady she ought to look less tired and fraught, but, as she said herself, being the head of a large school was no sinecure. A wave of illness had hit her staff, causing more problems.

Psychosomatic, she whispered to Stella as they apologized for being late. 'I can't blame them. With all this reorganization and a new Educational Authority in charge they are worried about their jobs. So they are hiding behind illness.' A 'flu-like one on this occasion.

Not the way worry took actors, Stella thought. They could be neurotic enough, as she well knew, but never would an illness keep them away from work. Whatever ailment brought on by depression infected them, they would get on the stage and perform. This was well known in the profession.

But, as now, stress showed in the way Lily Goldstone was complaining about her costume for the first act. 'I'm a bride, damn it,' she was saying to the wardrobe mistress. 'Just back from a honeymoon trip. I look like a mute at a funeral in this dress.'

It was actually a very attractive dress which she had praised the other day. Now she gave it a baleful stare and flung it from her. It was not needed, they were not dressing for the run-through and Lily was in her usual sweatshirt and jeans with *Up the Revolution* written across her chest. The wardrobe mistress carefully picked up the abused garment. She knew, and Lily knew, that Lily would be wearing it in Act One on the night.

JoJo Bell was going round offering herbal tea—this was her way of showing tension. Bridie was feeling sick, and Charlie Driscoll was telling anecdotes from his life—that was his.

On the whole, Stella thought, she preferred Lily's downright bad temper.

The first act was about to start and Stella stood up the better to be in command. She herself had a distinct ache and loss of strength in her right leg. If I was a dog, I'd drag it, she thought. She really must see a doctor when she had time.

They were playing a new translation of *Hedda Gabler*, one specially done for them, and in three acts. JoJo Bell, who played the aunt, and the girl who was both assistant stage manager and the maid in Act One, were standing ready.

Stella had assembled a strong but economical cast. She had to think of costs, of which salaries were the greater part. Lily Goldstone as Hedda was earning most, but even she had accepted a cut because she was living with Fergus Abbey, the young man who had done the translation.

Charlie Driscoll was Judge Brack, JoJo Bell was old Aunt Juliane, Will was the young philosopher, Eilert Lovborg, whose book Hedda destroys, while Bridie was Mrs Elvsted, the woman in love with him. Jorgen Tesman, Hedda's indestructible husband, was being played by Bob Tinker, an anxious bit of casting, because as well as being a name, he was also a drunk. But you had to take what you could get, Stella thought, and he was what she had got. At least long years and many playings together had taught her his little ways and what to look out for.

Not too much had been seen of him lately on the London stage because he had been filming (he acted just as well drunk or sober on film), but he was with them now looking pale and punctilious. She had heard he was into faithhealing, which ought to suit JoJo.

She walked forward, feeling miraculously strong now they were about to begin. Funny, her leg was fine now.

She consulted the plan of the scene on a pad before her. She was discovering herself to be one of those directors who have every move in every scene plotted out even before the first read-through. Needless to say, this tight control provoked fierce explosions from Lily Goldstone, who favoured a more spontaneous approach. The noisy arguments were much enjoyed by both parties, with the rest of the cast dividing fairly equally behind each protagonist.

Behind her, she was aware of John Coffin sliding into a seat next to Ted Lupus and Charlie's voice starting on his tale of a bottle of sherry (which was very far from being what it seemed) and a trifle and two other actors in Newcastle when he was in digs about twenty years ago.

The story itself must be a good hundred years older than that and had probably been going the rounds when David Garrick was on the boards.

She gave John Coffin a smile and a wave; he was almost punctual, half an hour late, she would settle for that. At that moment the bond between them was so strong that it overrode any sexual boundaries and stretched between them like a piece of ectoplasm, moving slightly in the hot air of the theatre, like a new organ joining their bodies. Coffin shifted uneasily in his seat.

'Let's get going then, JoJo.'

Enter MISS TESMAN *from the left carrying a letter.* THE MAID *is centre stage.*

MISS TESMAN: 'Why, I don't believe they are up yet.'

BERTA: 'That's what I said too, miss. But then the boat was so late in last night.'

The rehearsal got under way.

THOSE OF THE CAST not actually on stage at that moment sat around watching what was happening from a seat in the stalls, or drank coffee in their dressing-room, or just hung about waiting to make their entrance.

The decapitation of Peter Tiler was now common gossip among them, the subject of much speculation, some alarmed, some bawdy, none well informed.

Charlie Driscoll had abandoned his joke session and joined the backstage party.

'Cheer up, you two,' he said to Bridie and Will. 'This is a rehearsal, not a wake.'

A certain tenseness hung over all the cast, showing itself in a telling manner during Stella's pre-run-through talk earlier that evening.

'The police will want to speak to us all,' she had announced. 'Not sure when. About Peter Tiler.'

Dead silence greeted her. Lily Goldstone lit a cigarette, Bridie and Will moved closer to each other, and JoJo examined her nails. Little Billy, who was helping Max bring in the coffee and sandwiches, retired to a discreet spot to listen. He was so often about the place that he was taken for granted.

'Well, yes, we'd all rather not, but after all he did work here.'

'He was a swine and a pig,' announced Lily loudly. 'Do you know he tried to get money out of me? Blackmail. Got hold of some letters. I soon showed him the door. Publish and be damned.'

Silently the rest of the cast agreed that there was little in the way of revelations that could shame Lily. She was open in all she did. Peter Tiler had picked the wrong one there.

'He had a go at me too,' said Stella. 'Nothing very important, tried to hint I had been making a profit on the accounts.'

'Me too, as a matter of fact,' said Charlie diffidently.

'Really, Charlie? So what did you do?'

'Sent him away with a flea in his ear.'

'Good for you, Charlie.' No one asked him that which they all longed to know: what he had done that he could have been blackmailed for. After all, everyone had little matters they would prefer to keep quiet.

'Just as well he left when he did,' said Stella. 'Or he'd have got the sack.'

'So what do we do?' asked Charlie. 'Tell the police about the old bugger?'

'I ought to say yes,' said Stella. 'But I'm not your keeper. You're adults. Decide for yourself.'

Little Billy thought there were one or two other people who might have spoken but hadn't. He took a tin of Coke from the table. Grown-ups really were extraordinary. Peter Tiler hadn't *left*, he'd been murdered.

He took his can of Coke and went out to join the audience. He sat next to Ted and Kath Lupus. Kath knew him, he had been a member of her school before his parents despatched him to a smart prep school. That lad's been up to something, she thought. Sometimes Little Billy signalled things much more clearly than he knew. She gave him her professional, headmistress's smile, which he rightly interpreted as 'Watch it, I am on to you.'

When John Coffin arrived, Billy ran to offer him some coffee and sandwiches. 'You remember me, sir? I'm the one who found the head. And, sir, I know who did it.'

He whispered, but it was a stage whisper, and owing to the excellent training at the Baddeley School of Drama was distinctly audible.

'I'll talk to you later,' said Coffin, his eyes on the stage, where Charlie Driscoll was making a formidable Judge Brack, revealing a side of his character that one might not have suspected. Lily was magnificent as Hedda, malignant and powerful.

The assistant stage manager crept up and touched John Coffin on the arm. 'You're wanted on the telephone, sir.' She was impressed that there was someone so important in the house that he could be tracked down wherever he was.

On stage Hedda burnt the book written by her husband's rival, pretending it was her child; Judge Brack began the process of cold, sexual blackmail while her husband remained unaware; shortly Hedda would retire behind the curtain to shoot herself and the play would be over.

Coffin got up. 'Don't get lost,' he muttered to Little Billy, who looked surprised. He never got lost.

When Stella looked round as Hedda went behind the fatal curtain, she saw Coffin had gone.

THE HOUSE IN Hillington Crescent was bathed in the late evening sun. It had been a wet day which had now redeemed itself with steamy heat. Damp was rising from the heaps of earth in the garden. The policemen who had been digging it up had done their job well, back garden and front had been thoroughly turned over.

A uniformed constable stood at the gate, and Archie Lane was in the garden behind him. He saw Coffin looking at the bare earth.

'Disappointing, eh, sir?'

'You found nothing?'

'The remains of a dog, sir. Been there for years. Nothing else.'

The door of the house stood open and Coffin walked straight in.

In the hall, messy and earth-stained where a lot of feet had walked in and out, stood Superintendent Paul Lane. DI Young was in attendance.

Lane came forward. 'Just having a look round for myself. It alters everything, this bit of news.'

'So it was murder?'

'Yes. Perhaps you were expecting it.'

'I think I was. It didn't feel right.'

'Bill Baines rang me up as soon as he was certain. Mrs Tiler was murdered. Strangled and then hung up.'

'When? Can he say how long she has been dead?'

'The state of the body makes that difficult. But the neighbours put the last time she was seen as over fifteen days ago, memories are a bit vague. So between two and three weeks ago is as near as we can get at the moment.'

Coffin thought about it. 'And Tiler himself? I suppose he might have been killed about the same time.'

'Baines won't say yet.'

'We need to find the rest of the body.'

'Well, he isn't in the garden.'

A good idea that hadn't worked. The two people who had lived in this house had been murdered, but by whom and for what reason was still obscure.

'What about the house?'

'No sign of a struggle and no blood. Wherever Peter Tiler was killed, it wasn't here.'

'I'm going to have a look round.'

Accompanied by the other two, Coffin made a slow survey of the house. All the rooms were as he remembered them, but all now showed the marks of the police teams that had gone over them, searching and photographing. Never tidy, they now looked tumbled. If Mrs Tiler had been a keen housewife, as she might have been in her way, she would not have liked the state of her house now.

But she was dead, murdered, and so was Peter Tiler.

Coffin went back down the stairs and through to the kitchen. On the table was an old tin biscuit box.

'What's that?'

'The only thing we found that was interesting. Under the floorboards in the kitchen.'

Coffin looked inside the box. 'Photographs.' They looked as though they had been cut from magazines. They had a glossy shine to them that reminded him of something.

'All women. Young ones.'

'Dirty old man, was he?' asked Lane.

'Bit of a creep, sir.'

Coffin picked one up, handling it carefully because of fingerprints. A pretty blonde face stared out at him. 'I'd say these could have come from theatre programmes. Photographs of the cast, that kind of thing.'

Coffin went out into the garden. Slowly he walked down the narrow path, this garden had something to say to him and he wanted to read the message. A worm was sliding across a mound of freshly turned earth.

The black cat sat on top of the garden shed, eyeing him with expressionless yellow eyes.

Coffin went back up the garden path to the house, taking his time.

'What about the shed?' he asked Archie Young.

'Had a look round. Nothing much to see.'

'Dig it up. Go right underneath it.'

Without a word, the Inspector went out to the police car in the street and gave the orders.

Coffin sat waiting in the kitchen. Presently he was joined by Paul Lane. Archie Young stayed out with the diggers.

THE LIGHT FADED from the sky, lamps were rigged up in the garden to give the diggers light to see. The black cat removed himself to the safety of some bushes but remained around to watch.

Cats have memories, if no power to communicate them. And if he could have spoken what was in his mind, it would have been a catly memory. He remembered lights and movement and earth being dug once before, but what he chiefly remembered was the small furry animals that scuttered out disturbed and looking for fresh tunnels.

After a while, a man came out of the shed and spoke to Inspector Young, who turned and went back to the house.

'We have found a body,' he said to Coffin. 'About three feet down. But you're in for a shock. It's not Tiler. It's the body of a woman.'

Coffin followed Archie Young down the garden path. In the shed, by the yellow light from the lamp, he looked down into the hole. The girl lay on her back with her hands folded neatly on her stomach.

What was left of them, for natural decay and small animals had worked upon them. As with her face. But her hair was still golden and curly, although a potato was about to root itself in her heart.

Rosie Ascot was found.

SIX

THEIR HALF-BROTHER William, did not, after all, fall in with Lætitia's plans about where they should eat lunch. Instead, he wrote to her saying he would take them to Green's off Jermyn Street, he had heard the salad there was good.

'But this cannot be the reason,' observed Laetitia, as she passed on the news to Coffin. It was now Monday, three days after the finding of the second body in Hillington Crescent. The invitation was fixed for three days ahead, a Thursday. Coffin could attend, although the days between were busy and the finding of the body of the young actress and their complete failure to find the body of Peter Tiler had thrown the case wide open. 'Our brother is a dissembler.'

'It's in the blood,' answered Coffin, thinking of their mother who must have been the arch dissembler of all time. 'And he may just fancy champagne.' He had no idea of the surprise that William was about to spring on them. Nor that his brother was to prove, in the end, an acute commentator on the murder of Peter Tiler.

'I fancy it myself,' said Laetitia with a giggle. 'By the way, I do not think you are protecting my investment in St Luke's. Too much murder.'

'You're getting publicity.' This was certainly true. The papers for the last few days since the discovery in Hillington Crescent had been full of the case. Stella

Pinero had nervously identified the body as that of the missing actress but one famous daily paper was flying over from New Zealand Rosie Ascot's only relatives, an elderly aunt and uncle.

'But not the right sort.'

'The great British public loves murders, you know that.'

'I am bound to say that Stella tells me people are flocking to book.'

Years ago, and more than once since, Stella Pinero had complained that murder came too close to John Coffin. It was his job, granted, but was it also his fate? Arriving at the right place in time for the deed, just as a great artist is always there for the view, the theme, which he needs. An artist in crime? Stella found this disturbing.

St Luke's Mansions and the Theatre Workshop were certainly getting publicity now with three murders associated with them. MURDER THEATRE, was one newspaper headline. DEATH IN THE GARDEN, said another.

'But they all feel under suspicion,' complained his sister.

'They are under some suspicion. Can't be avoided.' To a certain extent every one connected with St Luke's, or with access to it, was under suspicion. Letty herself was probably being quietly investigated. And he would give something to know if there was a secret file on him. He had to assume there was.

Last night there had been a picture on the television news of Charlie Driscoll hurrying into the theatre, head down, looking furtive, and of Lily Goldstone staring defiantly at the camera and threatening to sue.

JoJo had managed to smile, while putting her arm in a protective way around Bridie's shoulders in a manner which succeeded in making the girl look terrified. Will just looked guilty.

Only Stella Pinero rose above it all. Years of publicity, some good, some bad, had given her a patina of protection. She smiled brilliantly, put on extra mascara and managed to see that every hair was perfectly in position. Coffin thought she was enjoying it, but on the telephone that morning she assured him she was not. 'I had all I wanted of death years ago in Greenwich when you and I first met, and I was young then. But I am an actress and can put on a show.' Which she certainly could. 'But you don't think I like the idea of that man's head in my flat for weeks?'

'We don't know how long,' observed Coffin mildly. 'Possibly not weeks.'

Stella was still staying with Charlie Driscoll who had a large and comfortable flat in Covent Garden, the perfect actor's home, he said, from which you could walk to almost any West End theatre if you happened to be lucky enough to be playing in one.

'Better still if you are an opera singer or a ballet dancer,' Stella had answered over their breakfast coffee. Charlie's last boyfriend, now on tour and suspected of having changed his loyalties, had been a dancer. As it was, they both came and went on Charlie's motorcycle, because the other thing he did not mention as a convenience of the Garden was that there was nowhere to park a car.

'Well, we are under suspicion,' she said as she returned from her telephone call with John Coffin. 'I taxed him with it—I love that word taxed, don't you, so descriptive—and he confirmed it. All the same, I don't think it's one of us, do you?'

'If it is,' said Charlie grumpily, 'then the next to go will be that boy Billy. The whole world must have heard him saying he knew who did it.'

'Oh, he's only a boy, Charlie. He can't know anything. Not really.'

'I've been a boy,' said Charlie. Which was news to Stella, as it was never clear what Charlie was or had been. He seemed able to be sexless or any sex, as all who had seen him in *Waiting for Godot* would testify. 'And I think he can.'

Stella came out with what really interested her. 'Then John Coffin asked me to lunch. At Green's. Some family party.'

'So what did you say?'

'I said No.' Stella drank some more coffee. 'But all the same, I think I shall move back into St Luke's Mansions.'

An apparent non sequitur that made clear sense to Charlie, who said to himself that the Poor Chap hadn't got a chance.

'Thanks for having me, Charlie. But I'm better living on the job.' Also the motorbike was chafing her legs and ruining her tights.

'You don't sound too miserable,' said Charlie suspiciously.

'Well, I am worried, and we are all under threat, and I felt it the more since it was my refrigerator and I had a key to that place, one of the policemen was quite sharp to me till I coaxed him round, but I've had a 'phone call from Letty Bingham and there might be good news on the way.' Stella gave her secret smile.

Good news meant good theatre news, they both knew that, there was no other sort of news that counted. Not even death and double murder.

Charlie, although he had a lot on his mind, decided to cheer up and bear it bravely. 'This is a far, far better thing that I do now than I have ever done,' he murmured to himself.

If all concerned with the Theatre Workshop felt under threat, Tom Cowley in his Black Museum perceived he had some cause for relief. The heat was off him and his museum. The powers that be had other things on their mind. In a quiet way, he rejoiced. An interesting, newsworthy local murder, the sort that gets written up, discussed at the Detection Club, lectured on at a Crimewriters' Conference and into the history books by way of a Notable British Trial, could do him nothing but good. An unsolved series of murders might prove to be an even greater attraction. Look at Jack the Ripper, never out of the paperback market; consider the Sydenham murders, some mileage there too, and there was even their own unsolved strangling whose relics he retained in the Black Museum. In due course he must manage, as curator, to lay his hands on a specimen piece of evidence from the case to mount on a display sheet and place in a glass cage. What about the head itself? Wasn't display what it was meant for? He smiled.

A certain fanaticism was beginning to show itself in his defence of his museum, alarming his wife, who was only slowly recovering from a nasty little illness herself and wondered if he was going down with something too.

Nor was she the only victim. Tom telephoned John Coffin, catching him at home in St Luke's Mansions on the very day of the family luncheon in Green's.

'You've heard about Dr Schlauffer? Yes, he's really bad, poor chap. There seems to be some sign of paralysis now. He's having trouble breathing. No, I'm better now. The wife's not too good, though. There's a nasty bug going round.'

'Which hospital is he in?'

'The Thameswater District. It's the new one down by the Isle of Dogs.'

'Are you all right yourself, Tom? You don't sound quite yourself.'

'Never felt better.'

But there was a brightness, a brassiness to his tone that Coffin did not like. He hoped old Tom wasn't going to go over the top. Uneasily he remembered that it was because of an incident in earlier days that Tom had been deposited in the sinecure of the Black Museum.

Later that day he arrived in Green's for the meeting he half dreaded. Letty was, as usual, late. But he had had no trouble recognizing his half-brother, they seemed to know each other without question.

'Drink? Let's start with champagne. After all, it's an historic moment, this meeting.' There was a Glasgow accent, slightly modified by Edinburgh, but more warmth than Coffin had expected.

He sat looking at his half-brother. William was younger than Coffin and older than Lætitia. But he could have been any age, he was ageless. There he sat, across the table, a tall, slender, sandy-haired man with spectacles, perfectly at his ease. Coffin tried to see something of his mother in William's face and could not. He wished he remembered her better.

'You were a surprise to me,' he said.

'It was a surprise to me, too. Although, of course, I knew I was adopted.'

'I don't understand how you ended up in Scotland.'

'I was fostered first. With a butcher's family in South London, so I understand.'

'I'd heard something about that,' said Coffin thoughtfully.

'But he didn't prosper. Or he died. I've never really been clear about that; I was only a few years old. Don't remember anything of it. So I was sent to his wife's sister in Glasgow. They were in a good way of business, but childless and they adopted me.'

Curiosity produced the next question. He must account for William somehow, he was so unlike both Lætitia and Coffin himself. His mother must have been a woman of catholic taste. But the father? What of the father? 'We both know who your real mother was, but do you know who was your father? Or anything about him.'

William shook his head, 'Nothing.'

'Lætitia knows about hers. I believe he's still alive.'

William looked thoughtful. 'It might be worth asking him a few questions.' A canny look came on his face, one that must have been familiar to his fellow Writers to the Signet in Edinburgh. 'But there again, some stones are best left unturned. I've found that in my business, and you must have done too.'

'I'm usually engaged in turning them over to see what crawls out,' said Coffin. He drank some champagne, looking around at the crowded room. William followed his gaze.

'I'm glad we came here. It was my wife's idea; she'd heard of it and wanted to see what it was like.'

'You've got a wife?'

'Of course.' William sounded surprised. 'Didn't Letty tell you? She's shopping in Harrods at the moment. She'll join us later. I thought we'd have this first bit on our own.'

Letty arrived at this moment. 'Sorry to be late. Business problems.'

'Your theatre? I told you there would be problems.' William was showing himself knowledgeable about this kin. 'Champagne?'

'Of course, and I'm going to eat lobster. You can eat salad on your own. Which of course, you never intended to do.'

'Ach, there's salad and salad,' said William, making what Coffin realized was an Edinburgh joke. 'When I said problems I did not think of murder, of course.'

'Who would? However, that was not what held me up.' Letty looked excited. 'No, I was on the telephone talking to a donor who is going to put money into the theatre. The big one, not the Theatre Workshop. Work is about to begin.'

'I thought I saw Ted Lupus in there this morning.'

'I'm pushing ahead. Sooner, much sooner than I expected. My donor, who wants to be anonymous, but I can tell you he is a big name in the industry, needs to see action. The money is coming to us in stages, as we show what we are doing. So we are starting to clear the ground. Literally, checking the foundations.'

'From the bottom up? You're not going to knock the church down?'

Letty laughed. 'It's not going to greatly change the church, it's a listed building, just kind of put the auditorium and open stage into the body of the kirk. But there's a lot of water underneath, we are near the Thames, after all, so we're going down into the foundations. We don't want the audience to go through the floor.'

'I suppose it has to be open stage?' Coffin was old-fashioned and enjoyed a stage with curtains and footlights. He wasn't looking for realism, just magic.

'I think so. But you'll like it. I've got a first-class man, a real genius of a theatre architect, Johnny Dunlop. You've heard of him? But Ted Lupus's outfit will be doing the construction. He was a bit surprised we were getting on so soon. I think he thought it would be years before we got the theatre proper going.' She added, 'I thought so myself at times.'

She leaned forward eagerly. 'I'm going to involve Stella Pinero in all this. She's such a magnetic person, such a draw. We shall need fund-raising shows, special performances, garden parties, the lot. I've already sounded her out. She'll do it. She's got a head on her shoulders.' Then she realized what she'd said. 'Oh, dear, a black joke now, isn't it?'

William showed he had read his newspapers. 'And of hands, too.'

'Right,' said Coffin.

'These hands and the head, they do belong to the same person?'

'We think so.' Coffin was surprised at the question.

'Then the head and the hand must have some special significance. Only one hand with the head. And Miss Pinero had the other. That's interesting, is it not?'

'Oh very, and don't think I haven't put it to myself.'

'Does someone not like Miss Pinero? Or is it you they are interested in? I think you will find that body, it does not matter to the murderer so he will not have worried too much where he put it.'

The arrival of the lobster salads prompted Letty to say, 'What about your wife? Won't we wait for her?'

'She'll mebbe not come if she's shopping.'

'Aren't you afraid she'll buy up Harrods?'

'Ach no, she's a sensible wee woman. And she thinks for many things Jenners is far better.'

Letty laughed. 'I think you told her not to come.'

'You'll meet her later, I trust, but I'll not deny I told her not to hurry. She's a bit of sceptic is my Winnie, and there were things I wanted to say.'

After they had eaten, William said: 'And now for the reason that I brought us here. You must have wondered when I would get to it.'

He drew out of his briefcase a leather-bound blue notebook. It was two or three inches thick. Not new.

'Yes, that's why I'm here. I found it in a case in the attic of the house in Glasgow. Must have been there for about twenty years. More, perhaps.'

'What is it?' asked Stella.

'It's a diary. Our mother's diary.'

'How did it get in the attic?' asked Coffin.

'I don't know for sure, nor how nor why, but I learnt after she was dead that she kept up with my adopted mother secretly over the years. They'd known each other as children. I think she must have meant this diary to be seen, perhaps for us to find it, and read it. I think she wanted the story to come out.'

A determined look came on William's face. 'And although my Winnie thinks it's pointless fuss and dead things should be left to lie, I think family loyalties count.'

It was sometime before John Coffin realized what a profoundly illuminating remark brother William had offered to him that day.

William laid the book on the table in front of him.

'Which of you will take it first?'

SEVEN

FOR TWENTY-FOUR HOURS and more, the case seemed frozen, with much work going on underneath but nothing appearing on the surface. Such periods came with every investigation, as Coffin very well knew. It was annoying to the Press, who needed development to fill their papers, and unnerving to all those involved.

The cast had been interviewed one by one, and had assisted or impeded the interrogation according to their temperaments and political beliefs. JoJo Bell had offered to help with the questioning as well as answering what was put to her, and had been surprised when she was turned down. Lily Goldstone had admitted that Peter Tiler had tried a touch of blackmail. No, admitted was not quite the word for Lily; announced, proclaimed, was more her style, and although many policemen, including several now in Coffin's new Force who had met Lily on various barricades and got the length of her tongue, would gladly have arrested her on the spot, there was no evidence to suggest she had killed Peter Tiler. Charlie and Stella had, more modestly, confessed to their brushes with the man, and hoped the matter had ended for them.

But in the Theatre Workshop, they had an added worry. The day after the lunch with brother William, Stella and Coffin met at the entrance to their respective front doors.

'I've got permission from your lot to move back in. Although why I should need permission to live in my own home I don't know.' She had three suitcases on the floor and a number of little bundles suspended, yet with extreme elegance, about her person.

'It's the forensics,' explained Coffin apologetically. 'They like to go over things. And photographs, they are important too.'

'See me in, will you? Just in case. I'm a bit nervous.'

In case what, Coffin wondered. 'Why didn't you hang on with Charlie a bit longer? You didn't quarrel, did you?'

'Oh, he's a sweet man. As bent as an eight-pound note, but sweet. No, we didn't quarrel, but it doesn't do to live with someone when you're working with them. Not for long, anyway. And I wanted to get back to my own place, even if it is a bit scarey.'

Coffin picked up two of her cases, both very, very heavy, just as he had known they would be. 'I don't think there'll be another body, Stella, or even a bit of one.'

'It might smell.' Stella left the other case for him to come back to and opened the door of her flat.

There was no smell but some disorder. Everything was slightly out of place and dusty.

'Good job I didn't have much furniture here. It will all need a thorough clean,' said Stella severely, as if she was or ever had been a housewife. 'That on top of everything else. Get the other case, will you?'

Coffin staggered under the weight of this one. 'What have you got in it, Stella?'

'Oh, just odds and ends,' she said vaguely. 'Not a body, if that's what's worrying you.'

'Now, Stella.'

She was taken with a sudden panic. 'Oh my God, a body couldn't have got in there without me knowing, could it? I left that case in the flat before I moved in.'

'You're acting, Stella.'

She had the case on the floor and was unlocking it. The lid sprang open, revealing domestic kitchen apparatus, like an electric kettle and a coffee pot, these representing as much of cookery as Stella aimed at these days. She began to take everything out, emptying the case until the floor all round her was littered with pots, pans, and a scrubbing brush which she looked at doubtfully. 'A long time since I've seen one of those. I think it must be Charlie's.' Then she sat back on her heels. 'Nothing dead. Thank God.'

'I'll clap, shall I? A good performance.'

She stood up, dusting her hands. 'Well, you asked for it. I owed it you. You didn't stay to watch our rehearsal.'

'And you know why.'

'Rosie Ascot's body, poor girl. Is that supposed to cheer me up? I keep thinking Who Next.'

'You'll be the first to know when we find Peter Tiler's body.'

'As if murder wasn't enough. It's not my only problem, I can tell you.' Stella was studying her face in a small pocket mirror. 'Look at me, I'm a wreck.'

'What else is there?'

'I need a total facelift.'

'Oh, come on, Stella, that's not it.'

'Perhaps it's my neck.' She was trying to pinch bits of flesh from under her chin. 'Yes, that's it. I could do with some of that cutting away.'

'Stella, you're still acting.'

She continued to study her face. 'Perhaps it's the chin. What do you think?'

'Stella, I'm off.'

She stopped playing and came out with her real worry.

'JoJo's ill.' She sounded exasperated. 'This illness is going to run through the whole cast, I can tell. They're working up for it.'

'She's got an understudy, hasn't she?'

'Oh, she'll probably insist on dragging herself on stage. I know JoJo.'

'Well then, you've got no problem.'

'And what's she going to look like? And what sort of a performance will she turn in?'

As good as usual, if not better, thought Coffin, who had learnt to know the ways of actresses. Drunk or sober, sick or ill, they could act. And would.

'Perhaps it's all Yuppie 'flu.'

'Have you seen JoJo, seen how she looks? Actresses don't have neurotic illnesses that spoil their looks. She's yellow, poor soul, and blotchy with it. The make-up girl is going to have a terrible job with her.'

'I suppose you know that Dr Schlauffer is very ill?'

'Of course I know. He was going to take me out to lunch, remember?'

'I think he might die.'

'I know that too. Oh John, I'm frightened.' She came closer and he put his arms round her. Her head rested on his shoulder. 'That feels better. I did need a bit of comfort. I'm all unnerved ... It's my first production, you see.'

'I understand.' Sickness, sudden death, murder, the odd body, that wasn't what was upsetting Stella, not really, only her work.

'And it's all going wrong.'

'I don't think so.'

She didn't answer.

'That's not the Stella I remember. The one that always fought back.' Not always very prettily, but never without spirit. His arms tightened around her. 'Is there anything else, Stella? Anything you're not telling me.'

'He was a foul man, that Tiler. Everything he touched has slime on it.'

He dropped his arms and stood a little back from her, studying her face. 'Do you know anything about his death, Stella?'

'No, nothing, of course not. What do you think I am? I thought you were supposed to be comforting me, not accusing me of murder.'

'Not exactly what I was doing.'

Grudgingly, she said: 'I might know where the pot came from.' She had decided to tell him something if not all. There were layers of truth in her mind about that pot.

'What pot?'

'The urn then, the one that had the head in it.'

'Oh.' He was surprised. 'Where?'

'Out back. In the sort of yard behind the Theatre Workshop where we store odds and ends.'

'How do you know it's the same pot? Did you ever see the urn?'

'One was there, and now it's not there.'

'How long was it there?'

'I don't know. I only just remembered it.'

'Anyone else notice it?'

Stella shrugged.

Probably not, he thought, but the question would have to be asked. The stage manager, professionally in the habit of noticing objects, might possibly have seen the urn.

'Thank you, Stella.'

'Oh, don't mention it,' she said jauntily, as if she felt better now. But she had not told quite all the truth.

They parted, Stella towards the theatre and Coffin on foot to his office.

As he walked toward Spinnergate Tube station, he was thoughtful. He had caught the faint whiff of dissimulation about Stella. When she was at her most spontaneous and most charming was when you had to watch her most. You always had to remember she was an actress.

Mimsie Marker was on parade as usual outside the Tube station with her newspapers on display on a little tray. As the district had changed, so had the papers on sale there changed. Now Mimsie had to supply papers described by her as 'nobs' papers, by which she meant such as the *Financial Times* and the *Economist*. She continued to maintain a good supply of vigorous and gossipy dailies, all of which she read herself.

She hastened forward, paper in hand, to offer to Coffin. She knew what he read and prided herself on performing this personal service for her 'regulars'.

'Poor old Tiler,' she said. 'So you've got his head and not the rest of him. That'd be like him, somehow.'

Coffin knew the extent of her local knowledge. 'Got any ideas where it could be, Mimsie?'

She shook her head. 'Not me. Can't help you there. But he was only a little fellow, so he wouldn't need a big hole.'

'Small, was he?' said Coffin. No one had told him that. 'You knew him, what sort of a chap was he?'

Mimsie pursed her lips. 'Seemed nice enough. Didn't notice him really.'

'Unobtrusive, would you say?'

'Quiet. Too quiet for his own good maybe.'

''Yes.' Coffin was thoughtful. 'That could be.'

'They were all quiet little men, the Tilers. Mind you, they were a funny lot. Not liked. Never liked, and yet you couldn't exactly see why. Of course, they had terrible bad luck.'

'They had?'

'Yes, well, Pete's father died in an accident at work, then his mother had a stroke. She hung around a long while, poor soul, but she wasn't up to much. 'Course it started before that, the grandpa was a proper tyke, I don't know what he didn't do, but it was the sort of thing that didn't get talked about when I was a girl. A nice father figure, he was. And the uncles were the same, from all I heard.' She took his money and gave him the change. 'But it was the same with all of them, cousins, nephews, uncles, the lot. Empty men. Some were drifters, some fairly ran on the rocks. No good.'

'What about the women in the family, the wives, mothers and sisters and so on?'

'Not any sisters, they ran to men in that family. And they always married doormats. From what I've heard,' finished Mimsie judicially, 'not the sort to make trouble, whatever they had to put up with.'

'Well, thanks, Mimsie, you've been a help.' He decided to prod a little bit more, he thought she had things to tell him. Whether she would or not was another matter. 'And did they have things to put up with?'

Mimsie showed no pleasure and no surprise either at this, but nodded reflectively. 'Yes, funny things happened in that family and most of them were kept hushed up.'

'That's not so unusual.'

'We've always done that round here, kept things to ourselves ... That's your train now, I can hear it.'

She couldn't possibly hear any such thing, he thought. Apart from the traffic noises, the train was well underground. He couldn't hear anything. 'What sort of funny things, Mimsie?'

She shrugged. 'Bit of cadging and pilfering, bit of arson. Bit of violent death and a bit of nasty sex. That sort of thing. I said that was your train.' She fixed him with an ironic gaze. 'Feel the vibrations in my feet.'

'And do the vibrations tell you which way the train is going, Mimsie?'

'Yes,' said Mimsie without a flicker of a smile. 'Clever feet, I've got. You don't want to miss it now, do you?'

And the maddening thing was that when he descended the escalator after this dismissal, it was his train in the station.

LATER THAT DAY, he made time to go and see Dr Schlauffer in the Thameswater District Hospital where he had been taken. The hospital was a big, handsome building, erected about ten years ago, architecturally bland but carefully planned to cut down cross-infections and to make both nursing and medical care simpler. Coffin thought it was a great improvement on the Victorian Poor Law institution it had replaced.

To his relief, Schlauffer was sitting up in bed and breathing normally.

'I'm glad to see you looking better.'

'They say I am coming on nicely.'

'Breathing all right now? Tom told me you were having trouble.'

'It threatened. You know, they tell I am having polio. But I say that this can't be. I had all the usual vaccines. We do these things well in Germany.'

'Of course,' said Coffin.

'Still, they say, this is what you have. Anyway, the same virus.' He sounded almost proud, as if he was a specimen case of unique value, even if the exact mechanism by which the virus had got to him was not yet understood. 'Somewhere you have caught it. Others also, I believe. And they are going to have an investigation of the source.'

Coffin did not stay long, leaving before he tired the German.

He went out into the corridor where he found himself face to face with a tall, blonde girl in a white coat. He read the name on her coat.

'Dr Nicholson?' he said hopefully.

She smiled and nodded as he introduced himself. He was a friend of the patient, knew him professionally.

'Dr Schlauffer seems much better?'

'I believe he is,' she said in an aloof way.

'Don't you know?' Coffin was surprised at the off-hand comment. 'Surely you can tell?'

Dr Nicholson smiled. 'He is not my patient. I am an epidemiologist investigating the case. It's quite a nice little problem he has given us.' Her smile increased in brilliance as she produced her notebook. 'If you are a friend of Dr Schlauffer, then I must take your name and address. You may be an important witness. I shall probably want a blood sample from you. Yes, why don't we get that done now?'

A few minutes later, minus a small quantity of blood, and with the suggestion that more unmentionable samples from him might be required should his blood provide interesting evidence, Coffin drove back to St Luke's Mansions. Schlauffer was getting better; he himself felt much worse.

'It's a circle,' he said as he coped with the traffic flowing all around him. 'He's a case, and I'm a witness. We are all a witness in someone else's case.'

Or were ourselves a case, that was the other side of it. Even the cocky Dr Wendy Nicholson (he had read that name too) was a case to someone. He found that thought cheering.

As he passed the Spinnergate Tube station he saw Mimsie by her paper stall, sitting down this time, wearing a fine feathered hat. He got out to buy an evening paper.

'About Peter Tiler, Mimsie. Any more to say?'

She hesitated. 'When I was a kid, they said they had a ghost in that family. A kind of evil spirit that moved around with them.'

'What sort of ghost?'

'The sort of ghost that puffs itself up into old clothes, and throws furniture about and lights fires that don't burn anything. So I heard. All tales, maybe.'

A poltergeist, thought Coffin. That reflected a disturbed family.

'My gran said she saw it once when she was a kid. It was sitting on the doorstep, looking like an old overcoat and waving its arms at her.'

'Really?' It was an interesting insight into the superstitions and beliefs of the Docklands in the 1890s. No wonder Jack the Ripper did so well.

'She was the one who said it got into them all. Like a kind of infection. Remember her saying it.'

'Did you think that too?'

Mimsie laughed. He got no direct answer. Perhaps she did, perhaps she didn't.

Finally she said, in a hoarse whisper: 'People don't have that sort of thing, do they?'

Possibly not. But if anyone was going to, wouldn't it be a man born to have his head cut off?

THE ENTRANCE HALL where he had parted from Stella that morning was empty, but a note on the door suggesting that the milkman leave a pint and a breath of her scent suggested that she had passed through.

Beyond the door that led to the main church, he could hear voices. Ted Lupus came through the door, brushing dust from his jacket.

He noticed that Ted Lupus had a black armband round his sleeve. You didn't often see one of those these days. Ted saw him looking.

'A death in the family,' he murmured.

'Oh, I'm sorry. A close relative?'

'No, distant.' Ted hesitated. 'It's a mark of respect. Memory, really.'

Letty followed him through the door, accompanied by a burly man with a youngish face and what must be a prematurely greying beard whom she introduced as her theatre architect. He appeared to be completely under Letty's control.

'We are having a look at the crypt floor, seeing what's underneath. Ted wasn't keen, said we should wait a bit. I didn't know there was a season for digging up floors but it seems there is. Something to do with the water table.'

'If it's what you want, Mrs Bingham.' Ted Lupus sounded resigned. It was a tone that Coffin had heard before from those working with his sister.

'It's what I want.' Letty was decided.

'I think it's all right to get on with it,' said the architect easily. 'I need to get to know all the problems.'

'We have to look at the foundations, Ted,' said Letty.

'Couple of men down there now.'

'The floor of the crypt took a whack in the war.' To the young architect the war was not even a memory, just a piece of history.

'Fire bomb, I believe.'

'And they only did a rough tidy up job after that?'

'Nothing else seemed necessary then.'

'Right,' said Letty. 'And now it is.'

'Smells pretty earthy down there,' said Coffin. 'I've noticed it about the place. Seems to hang around.'

'You always get a smell in these old places,' said Ted Lupus.

Coffin picked up his briefcase and got out his doorkey. 'Come up and have a drink, all of you, when you're through.'

He left them, Letty giving tongue on some aspect of theatre planning while her architect murmured politely, and, opening his front door, he climbed his winding staircase, reflecting as he mounted the stairs that if he stayed in this place into old age, he would have to put in a lift. He could imagine the sort of old man he might become: difficult and irritable, with a tendency to prose. Then he laughed. Life never turned out the way you expected. He might not get an old age. He had come very close to sudden death in his life once already.

Stella and Letty, of course, would never age. It was something built in their genes. What you inherited was what counted. Later, when he got from Letty their mother's diary, then he might know a bit more about his own chances. Letty had been very cagey so far about revealing what she had read. Interesting and amusing, she had said briefly. It could not be a question of style. He doubted if his mother was a literary stylist, so it must be have to do with the matter.

He was getting ice out of the refrigerator when his bell was rung loudly. Then again.

'Coming, coming,' he called, hurrying down. They were very eager for their drink.

Letty stood there alone. 'John, you'd better come with me. The workmen have found something.'

Ted Lupus and the architect stood looking down at an area of the crypt floor from which the paving stones had been lifted. A third man, who appeared to be the site foreman, was with them. The two men who had been working there stood to one side. A strongly unpleasant smell was seeping into the air, colouring the damp earthiness already there with something nastier.

Coffin looked down. He saw a thick and suggestive-looking bundle, covered in an earth-coloured paper, tied up with rope. Through the paper, he could see what looked like a striped blanket.

He knelt down to study more closely what was there. A squarish, thick bundle. He thought it was a body. Certainly it smelt like one.

He put out a tentative hand to feel what he had: solid yet yielding, a strange sensation. Delicately, he traced out what could be an arm, a leg, hard to be sure which since the limbs had been bound together. Trussed up like a chicken.

Coffin stood up and drew back from the excavation. 'I'll get this looked at. You'll have to hang around. Sorry about that.'

He turned towards the narrow stairs that led up from the crypt.

'Sir.' One of the young workmen spoke up. 'Was this crypt ever used as a burying place? Legit, I mean. Proper funerals.'

'I don't know. Why?'

The young man walked to the end of the area where they had been working. The floor was very broken, not all the old paving stones had survived the war, and of those that had many were cracked and in pieces. One or two of the remaining stones had already been levered up.

'We had a go here first, before the foreman told us to move down the room a bit to where we found what we did. But before that I saw this: look here.'

A small object could be seen through a thin veil of earth.

'Is that a finger, sir? Is that a hand?'

EIGHT

A THIN SKIN of earth lay over the newly discovered body. The bundle which contained the trunk and limbs of Peter Tiler had been given a shallow burial place at the other end, as if he had no connection in life or death with what lay so close.

As he may not have had. There was no indication that the person who had buried this wrapped-up torso had known about the body next door. There was some slight suggestion that he or she had not. The Tiler parcel had been covered with earth and a paving stone placed on top. The other body was hardly interred at all. The style was different, said the police team. And if the burier of Peter Tiler had known of the other body, would he (or she, as the case might be) have bothered to set up such a careful disposal, stone and all? They thought not.

So they were thinking of two different killers, were they? speculated John Coffin.

The second body was carefully, painstakingly uncovered like an archaeological find. A small brush was used to remove the last crumbs of soil. Even the soil itself was carefully bagged to see what it might contain of evidence.

They had found the skeleton of a woman. Almost all the flesh had melted away, but clothes remained. She had been wearing jeans and a shirt, so there was nothing archaic about this lady. The exact dating of her death remained open, to be discovered, but a piece of newspaper caught up in her clothing would be offered up for dating and might yield a result. The one thing that could be said at this stage was that she had been dead considerably longer than Peter Tiler. She had predeceased him by some years.

Another conclusion appeared also. It was suspected by experienced police officers that Peter Tiler had died after his wife. Scattered over his clothes were the dried remains of several flying ants. These winged insects had appeared only for a brief two weeks that summer, then disappeared. From other calculations they believed Mrs Tiler had died before they arrived.

Superintendent Paul Lane, the one in supreme command of the investigation, and now taking an increasingly active part in it, on which he or DI Young made daily, sometimes hourly, reports to John Coffin, stood by watching as the workers uncovered the body of the woman who had been wearing blue jeans and a white shirt. The cause of death was as yet unknown but he was going to take a bet that she had been strangled by the stocking round what had been her throat.

He ordered the whole floor of the crypt to be lifted, layer by broken layer.

The first results came soon. A muffled exclamation from a pair of men working together, then silence.

In this way was the third body discovered. Buried in much the same way as the second. Another woman.

And yet another.

Then one more.

In all there were four bodies of women buried under the floor of the crypt. The time-span of their deaths had yet to be established, but it was conjectured by those doing the digging that they had all died within the last ten years. Maybe more, maybe less, but there would not be much in it.

That was what the diggers and the observers said to each other, and they did not expect to be proved wrong. It was how it looked.

John Coffin received the now almost minute by minute reports soberly. He knew that his new Force had a major investigation on their hands.

He had another worry also, one which he shared with the medical scientists in the area. They were studying the wave of polio cases of varying degrees of intensity, the epicentre of which appeared to be the Black Museum. One after another of the victims was turning out to have been at the party in the Museum or to have been in close contact with those who had.

It's a funny old world, thought Coffin, who had to bear all this in mind, as well as the other things he knew of, such as the IRA cell said to be moving into his district, and the witches' coven reputed to be working there already (white witches, they said, not black, as if that made it better), and the plans for a Royal visit with which the other two arrivals might or might not be connected. Take your eyes off it for a moment and it got away from you.

THE BODIES WERE NOW in mortuary drawers and labelled:

Body One. Female, probably aged between twenty and thirty. Hair colour, fair. Height in life estimated to be 162.5 cm. (around 5 feet 4 inches). Weight, hard to estimate, but a small frame made a guess of 60 kilograms or about 130 lbs give or take a bit reasonable. Teeth in good condition but several extractions.

Body Two. Female, probably under twenty. Hair colour, dark brown. Height in life estimated to be 160 cm. or 5 feet 3 inches. Small frame. Weight, a possible 62.3 kilograms (138 lbs). The left leg half an inch shorter than the right. Probably wore a built-up shoe.

The pathologist noting down this fact raised his head and spoke his thought aloud: 'That ought to make identification easier.'

If she left a shoe around. Cinderella, come forward.

Body Three. Female, probably between twenty and thirty. Hair, light brown. Height, 177.5 cm. A tall girl, about 5 feet 10 inches. Large frame. 80 kilograms. (176 lbs).

Body Four: Female, probably between thirty and forty. Hair, light red, probably dyed. Height, 165.0 cm. 5 feet 5 inches. Weight, medium frame, estimate 64 kilograms (141 lbs).

At this stage, there were few other personal details he could add. More might emerge later.

NINE

ON THIS BRIGHT summer's day, some thirty-six hours after the discovery of the row of female bodies, Max had set tables under an awning outside his shop where he was busy serving coffee and breakfast to such as desired it. The bemused cast from the Theatre Workshop had assembled there for support and company. Charlie Driscoll, JoJo Bell (looking pale but bravely protesting she was better), Lily Goldstone in jeans and Katherine Hamnett shirt, together with Bridie and Will carefully not holding hands, were seated at adjoining tables. Deirdre Dreamer was not present: she was ill, the latest victim to the mini-epidemic, while another absentee, Roger Clifford, was away filming. Ellie Foster was present, but silently drinking whisky in her coffee with a determined look. A bad sign for her sobriety to all those who knew her well. Stella herself was there, looking white and shocked. What to do? she was thinking, and then, the next minute: I cannot believe there's a connection. And I told Johnnyboy about the pot. Or urn. Well, I told him a bit, even if not all. Johnnyboy, or John Coffin (who had always hated being called Johnny), was not present, nor did she expect to see him. She had heard him leave his apartment in the tower at an early hour that morning.

Upon this little band had fallen the worst of the shock of the bodies in the crypt of St Luke's. All rehearsals had been cancelled, crash barriers set up on the road outside the church while police teams had moved in.

The barriers were there with a reason, already the crowds stood two deep, and several TV camera teams had arrived. A hot dog stand and an ice-cream van had trundled into position. The theatre group felt they were lucky that Max had reserved the tables for them, but on the other hand they were in the public eye.

They were performers, they loved publicity, but this was too much. 'We're a spectator sport,' groaned Charlie. He cuffed away a small girl who had crept through the crowd and attached herself to his leg.

'Papa, Papa!'

'I'm not your papa. I shouldn't think you've got one. You were fathered in a forest, my dear.' Charlie did not like children. 'Stella, do something. Protect me. I am your responsibility.'

'Take no notice of her, she's a midget from the Adlon Circus School. She's looking for publicity.'

It was indeed the case that the TV cameras were swivelling their way. The Tideway Morning TV team had the reputation of liking a ribald joke. Stella recognized one of their outfit and she suspected that Charlie did too. He knew the joke was on him, and probably why. Surely his last boyfriend had worked for Tideway before leaving in a huff for the fresh fields of New York? He and Chris (the lad had been called Chris) had worked on a soap for Tideway, in which they had played father and son. Stella had been in a few instalments herself, but she was no good on TV, couldn't do it and looked too fat. Oh God, that word again. Fat, fatter, fattest, the very word was like a knell.

'She'll get more than that from me. Hop it.' Morosely Charlie drank some coffee and crumbled a roll. 'Did I ever tell you about the time I was in panto in Torquay with a troupe of performing monkeys? *Robinson Crusoe*, you can put anything that moves and raises a laugh in *Crusoe*. Or so our producer thought. I've never hated anything in my life like that pissing troupe. She has a distinct resemblance to the leader of that little lot.' Another small creature had succeeded in making her way through the crowd. 'My God, here's another of them. They're a troupe.'

'Papa, papa!'

'Push off.'

'Can't you see they're pulling your leg? Someone has been watching *Der Rosenkavalier*.'

Charlie was no opera-goer and did not take the allusion. 'I believe they've been paid to do it. Go away, you nameless horrors.'

One of his small assailants said: 'I'm Lotty, she's Trishia. Buy us a drink and we'll stop.'

'It's too early to drink.'

'Just white wine. I don't count that.' Lotty pulled up a chair and clambered on to it. She was a lively-faced lady with bright red hair and the face of a clown.

'You shouldn't be doing this sort of work,' said Charlie irritably.

'Why not? I've got my Equity card, the same as you, and I bet I get more work.'

'That wouldn't be difficult.' Charlie looked towards the shop. 'Oh, all right, wine it is, then.'

Little Billy, who had managed to insert himself into the act, trotted away to do his order. He was there so much that no one took any notice. Sometimes they saw him, sometimes he felt invisible.

'Things aren't so bad,' said Stella, determined to cheer up her company. 'The police say we can get back into the Workshop tomorrow and the rehearsal can go forward. First night won't need to be postponed or anything.'

'Unless we're all in the nick.'

'Rubbish.' Stella burst into a peal of delicate laughter, culled, if that was the word, as she realized as soon as she gave vent to it, from her performance as Judith Bliss years ago. She had been acting that part too often lately, she must give it a rest.

'Stella duckie, do you have to be so bright and cheerful?'

'Oh, come on, Charlie, I can't bear you when you are so full of self-pity. Buck up.'

'Buck up, she says. Corpses all around us, the police breathing down our necks and she says buck up.'

'They can't suspect us of killing any of those poor girls.'

'There is still the murder of Peter Tiler,' Charlie reminded her sourly. 'Someone did him in, and with several of us admitting he tried to blackmail us, I would say we were prime candidates for that one.'

'But all those other bodies...' began Stella.

'Stella, I know you are not a great brain, but I should think that even you could see that there does not have to be a connection between their deaths and Peter Tiler's.'

'I don't believe in coincidence,' said Stella stoutly. 'All the deaths have to be part of the same process. And nothing to do with us. Those girls were killed long before the Workshop was even thought of. I shall say so if I'm asked.'

She did not reassure Charlie.

'Put a rope round my neck, won't you, while you're about it? I grew up around here. Don't forget that. So did a number of others of your cast. There is a policy of employing actors with local connections, remember? JoJo Bell went to school here, Bridie and Will still live here, even Lily's old grandpa ran the local cinema before they all went up in the world. I hear he's still alive.'

'Connections, connections,' said Lily, projecting her voice like Regan attacking King Lear. 'How dare you? As a good Marxist, Grandpa would not dream of doing anything so capitalist as killing four girls.' It was from her grandfather that Lily got her politics.

'I'm not accusing your grandfather of anything.'

'Thank you.'

'The rest of us now, that might be different.'

JoJo, still looking weak and tired but protesting she was fine, fine, and that her life had been saved by large doses of vitamin E in liquid form, murmured that she had been ten when she left the district and although her brothers still lived here, they were not murderers, and women did not kill women.

'You believe so?' asked Charlie ominously.

'Charlie,' said Stella in warning. 'Watch what you're saying.'

'Well, it's irrelevant, what JoJo says. Women do kill women. We don't know yet who these poor creatures were and why they killed. But we do know how the police mind works. They'll pick on one of us. So that's what he was blackmailing you about, they will say. So that was why you killed him. To hide all the women you've done in. Perverted sex, that'll be their line, and whether we're male or female or just mixed up like me won't really count.'

Bridie gave a little scream.

Stella patted her arm. 'Don't worry, dear, he's just being silly. You have got a nasty tongue on you, Charlie.'

'I see things straight.'

With dignity, Stella addressed such of the cast of *Hedda* as was assembled. 'I want you all to know that I believe you all to be innocent.' And to herself she said: 'Because I suspect someone else.'

She knew her cast, knew that they were just acting out their fears, and knew also that their performances in *Hedda* would not suffer. For the moment, Max's shop was their stage, and in different degrees they were enjoying their performances.

But she was well aware that there was another drama going on behind the arras. 'I'll have to tell John about who was carrying the urn. He will probably say it means nothing,' she said to herself. 'But I'll find my moment.'

OFFSTAGE, John Coffin was preparing a paper he was obliged to present to a committee of the House of Commons on the nature and future of the Force he was in the process of creating. It was because of his eloquence on the subject at a selection board eighteen months ago that he had got the job he now enjoyed.

That and his remarkable record in past years, together with the backing of his superiors in the Met. They had actively campaigned for him to get the job. 'An outstanding officer,' the Commissioner had said. 'The only officer with the vision to create a new force.' Now he wondered if they expected him to fail.

But that was cynicism above and beyond the call of duty, brought on by his present labours, and must be disregarded. He had a job to do in this area and it was his to do well.

He was writing in longhand, because his thoughts ran freer that way, but all around him he had reports and statements and surveys from the various bodies he had called upon for information. Advice he had not asked for, but advice they had all given him, sometimes tactfully, sometimes with a heavy hand. Where he wanted facts, they offered opinions. He took a deep breath and began again a paragraph he had already started twice.

His work had already been interrupted by an anxious telephone call from his sister, Letty Bingham. She was in New York with her husband and complained that she felt far away and helpless while her pet project fell apart. She might lose money, too, this was terrible. And she had her daughter's future to think about. What was he doing about it? It was up to him. It was Letty at her worst.

'What's going on? All those bodies! I don't like it. I'm coming over.'

Probably she was on her way back now. Letty, in defence of her own ends, was a formidable woman. She must take after their mother, about whom he hoped to know more when Letty handed over her diary for him to read. The thought of his mother made him stop work.

He went to his window and looked out. What he wanted to think about was not his mother, not this report, but the dead woman in St Luke's church. Who were they, where had they come from and how had they died?

Lists of missing women from all over the country were being studied now. He knew that the police scientists would be working to establish how they died, and how long ago. After this, the police machine might be able to move on to give them names.

One name they knew, Rosie Ascot. But Coffin also knew there was a chance that the others might never be given an identity.

He considered the problem.

What did they have so far? Five bodies. Seven, when Rosie Ascot and Mrs Tiler were counted in. It made for a complicated picture. Six dead women and one dead man.

They had the death of Mrs Tiler who had apparently been killed before her husband. They had the murder of Peter Tiler. They had this accumulation of dead women. Mrs Tiler had been strangled. So had the women. This was not a hard scientific fact yet, but he had seen the scarf round one dead throat. So Mrs Tiler and the other women had died in the same way.

Was there a connection between all the deaths? The murder of Rosie Ascot suggested there was. Killed in the same way as Mrs Tiler and probably the other women, and buried in the Tiler garden. They did not, as yet, know how Peter Tiler had been killed.

So they might have one murderer, or two murderers, or even three.

While he went back to what he was writing, his mind gnawed away at the problem.

The urn or bronze pot had indeed been seen at the theatre. Several people had admitted noticing it in the small yard at the back of the Theatre Workshop. The stage manager and the property mistress denied knowing anything about it. It had been there and then had not been there.

That bloody urn, thought Coffin. It had to mean something. When this case was sorted out, the reason for the urn would show itself.

But it tied one murder into the Theatre Workshop. As did the murder of Rosie Ascot.

Rosie Ascot had been buried in the Tilers' garden shed, and the owner of the shed himself, Peter Tiler, or what was left of him after decapitation, had been hidden in the crypt of St Luke's.

But the link had been there from the beginning. Peter Tiler had worked in St Luke's and the urn with his head in it had been addressed there.

It had to be admitted that several of Stella's theatre group were local people.

In his paper he had come to the section where he stressed the importance of understanding and maintaining the network of family relationships in the old boroughs of Leathergate, Spinnergate, Swinehouse and Easthythe, and perpetuating them in the new unit. (One reason, Tom Cowley said, for carrying on the Black Museum; they were proud of their history round here, even the blackest bits.)

Just for a moment Coffin's attention was diverted to his own family network. What would he find when it came to be his turn to read his mother's diary?

He raised his head from what he was writing. His conversation with Mimsie Marker on the subject of the Tiler family flashed into his mind. There was something to dig up there.

Might remind Paul Lane and Archie Young to look into the family relationships of all concerned in this case.

Even Stella Pinero? Yes, even Stella, although she was as free of family connections as any woman he had ever known. She had a daughter, but one never saw her.

Prompt on her cue, as always, she telephoned.

'You don't mind that I have telephoned?'

'Of course not.'

'I thought you sounded annoyed.'

'Just surprised.' I was thinking of you and you telephoned. I do think about you, and far too much, Miss Pinero. Stella. Or, as it might be, darling.

'It's just I've been mulling this over all day, wondering whether to tell you. I decided I must.'

'So what is it?'

'It's about the pot, the urn. I saw it in the yard of the Workshop.'

'Yes, that's confirmed. Others saw it too.'

'Oh, you checked?' She was a little chilled at his professionalism. 'Well, I saw Bridie carrying it away. That's what I had to tell you. She had it in her arms and was carrying it as if it was heavy.'

'I see.' Bridie? Yes, the pretty, worried-looking creature so firmly anchored to her young actor. 'Have you said anything to her?'

'Well, yes.'

'It might have been better not to.'

'She just denied it.'

'And you don't think you are mistaken?'

Stella would have none of that. 'Why do you imagine I've been fussing all day? I know what I saw. And Bridie was upset when she denied it. She covered up; after all, she can act, and not badly, but she couldn't fool me. Besides, she looks ill.'

'You don't think she *is* ill?' Going down with whatever this disease was. A virus infection, they were calling it. More reports about the epidemic were filtering on to his desk, adding to his worries. Everything pointed to the Black Museum as an important centre of the infection. The words Virus Mechanism (they seemed to merit capitals), were beginning to haunt him.

'Not that way. In the mind,' Stella was short.

'Right. You leave it now, Stella. I'll get someone to question her.'

He put the receiver down and went back to work.

It had to be a man's crime, though. Women did not do such things.

IT WAS ONLY AFTER a prickly interview with his parents that Little Billy had got permission to join his friends of the Theatre Workshop. Since it was his half-term holiday, he was a free man, so why not? But his mother was nervous of his safety, she didn't like all these murders and there was a lot of sickness about, while his father thought if he was going to be around there so much and doing so many odd jobs as well, then he ought to get paid for it. Negotiate a rate, was his advice.

But, although absent-minded parents with their minds on other things, such as Keith Larger's new factory and the sale of the apartment in Spain and, in his mother's case, her new clothes for Ascot, they were also loving and indulgent, so with very little pressure from him, Billy got their permission to hang about his friends on condition he was home for supper. He would probably have gone anyway, having come to a silent compact with the au pair that if she wouldn't say, he wouldn't say either. He knew all about her boyfriend who worked for Ted Lupus.

For their part, the cast of *Hedda Gabler* were so used to his constant presence that they took him for granted. Moreover, he was useful: he would run errands, make coffee, go round to Max's for sandwiches and cold drinks, take telephone messages and give cues if one of them wanted to run through their lines. Little Billy himself reckoned that he knew everyone's lines and could have acted every part. In imagination he did just that. The role he preferred was, naturally, that of Hedda. The young poet Lovborg was wet.

After the breakfast coffee at Max's it was an anxious, tense day on which the cast hung around the Workshop, avoiding the police as much as possible while trying to get support from each other.

Little Billy was the silent, interested spectator at several uneasy interviews. He watched from behind a piece of scenery (the dark porcelain stove of the Tesman drawing-room, Act One, *Hedda Gabler*) while Stella had a short but worried talk with Ted Lupus. As far as Billy could follow, Ted was explaining how the building operations would be held up while the police investigation went on, but he would make up for lost time as soon as he was permitted. Gloomily, Ted expressed the hope that he would not lose some of his best workers because of their inherited dislike of the police.

'People round here don't like being questioned, Miss Pinero,' Billy heard him say. 'Can't say I like it myself.' He sounded depressed.

Shortly after this, Billy carried a chair for Stella to sit on while she took a long telephone call from Letty Bingham in New York. Mrs Bingham was flying back to take charge. He heard that much before Stella glared at him and he left.

Charlie Driscoll was heard consulting JoJo as Equity rep and Lily Goldstone, who was well up in these things, about the legal services due to Equity members if arrested. He gave Little Billy, who was helping the stage manager with her props by moving the bookcase from Act Two from one spot to another, a stern look saying, Hop it, you. Billy moved away behind the bookcase where he could still hear and not be seen.

Resting here, and chewing an apple, he heard JoJo on the office telephone talking to her homeopathic doctor, and Ted Lupus having a conversation with his wife. All was grist to his mill.

Later, carrying lettuce sandwiches in for JoJo, the boy observed Bridie and Will muttering in a corner. He met Bridie's troubled eyes and wished he hadn't.

Better give them a wide berth in future. Hear no evil, see no evil, he thought.

Everyone saw him, no one saw him.

For some time now, Little Billy had been uneasy himself. It had been unwise to say he knew who killed Peter Tiler. Let himself get carried away there, he had, but it had been stupid. He considered talking to his father and decided against it. Go straight to police. Speak to John Coffin tomorrow. After all, he, Billy, was an important witness, he had helped find the head in the urn.

Slowly the theatre emptied. People had hung around for company and because they were miserable, but now, one by one or in groups, they were drifting off.

Because of the heat following a period of rain, a white mist was growing up as evening came on. Nearest the river it was dense.

Little Billy made his way home through it with his mind on the sausages and chips that Karen, the au pair, had promised him for his supper. He felt a bit queasy actually, not really up to sausages. He had a really bad headache, too.

As he turned towards the river, passing an old factory in the process of being reconstructed into luxury maisonettes, he thought he heard footsteps behind him. They seemed to keep pace with him. Well, he could guess who it might be.

Not really frightened, he slid behind a large builders' skip filled to overflowing with rubbish. He crouched there, eyes on the ground, waiting for the feet to pass.

The footsteps came on. He could see the feet beneath the edge of the skip. High heels. A woman.

Then he realized that he was very frightened, because it wasn't who he thought it was behind him. And he knew those shoes. This person was very difficult to protect himself from. This person had power.

Feeling sick, he decided he must hide. He knew a hiding-place.

TEN

THE UNWINDING OF the case began at a time when Little Billy had just gone into hiding but before his parents knew he was missing. Before Bridie and Will had been questioned, but when tension, even anger was growing between them.

Most major investigations reach this point, a climax, from which they gradually unwind. Those that do not are the failures, the cases where the file is never closed.

In this case, now known in the press as the Spinnergate Murders, the process began in a bedsitting-room overlooking the river. Not a smart room, but with a cosiness that reflected the tenant. Pink curtains with a matching frilly bedcover, a fluffy bedside mat of some unidentified long-haired animal, and a comfortable armchair in front of a large television set. There was scent on the air, a strongly floral smell with a lot of rose and a touch of hyacinth. The owner of all this was sitting at her dressing-table, also well frilled, wearing a satin housecoat with fluffy mules on her feet. Such an outfit had represented luxury to her as a teenager and still did, although she was, in many ways, a highly sophisticated lady.

She was talking to herself. She was also putting mascara on her lashes.

'Oh, you do make me laugh, Paulie.' But she was not laughing, conspicuously not laughing, not at all. 'You do have silly thoughts.'

Pauline Cochran, a woman not known to John Coffin, although he had her name on a list somewhere, but known to a number of people connected with the case.

She sat back, studying her face in the glass on her dressing-table. 'I'm not sure if this mascara does anything for me.' It was silvery blue, tipping her lashes with bright colour. She put her head on one side. 'Paulie, you know you've got to say. To someone.' She put on another layer of mascara to see if that improved things, her lashes looked like a fly's legs now, thick and iridescent. Not bad. 'The truth is, you'd rather not, wouldn't you? Let's be honest.' She held out her hand to see how her nail varnish was holding up. The deep rose tips seemed unscratched. 'You know what your mother would say? Keep your nose out of it, that's what Mum would say.' She had erected her mother, now dead, into a sort of oracle figure, although in life she had never consulted her at all. 'I mean, the police aren't exactly a girl like you's best friend.' But curiosity and a kind of obstinacy drove her on.

She finished her make-up job, then dressed to go out. She did not have a telephone in her room, but there was a pay-phone in the hall which all the tenants used when it was working.

'Amelia? There's something I think you ought to know.'

Amelia Marr, the proprietress of an establishment of discreet ill-fame in a street near the Tube station, listened. Her taste in rooms ran to blue with touches of gold because that was welcoming and pleasing was her trade. 'Oh dear. Are you sure, Paulie?'

''Course I'm not sure. Not being a detective and an identifier of dead bodies rolled into one, but I think it could be her. As soon as I heard about all those dead women being found, I thought: One of those could be her.' The district grapevine had worked fast. 'I bet I'm right. Mind you, I don't know which one.'

'But I thought she said she was going back home to Durham?'

'That's what she said, but I don't think she ever went. I've still got her pale mink stole she lent me to go to *Les Mis'* in.' They were a classy lot, Mrs Marr's girls, and liked a musical with a bit of social comment. 'And I know she'd have come back for that.'

'I think you're right, dear.'

'I know I am. So what do we do?'

'Leave it to me, dear,' said Mrs Marr. 'I'll put my thinking cap on.'

Not much thinking was required, and although it nearly broke her heart to cooperate with them, she telephoned the police.

'Not that the young CID chap I spoke to was much use,' she said later that day to Mimsie Marker, everyone's friend and universal confidante. 'But I suppose he took it in. In my position it wasn't so easy to speak up, you know, I have to be so careful, and keeping quiet is usually the best way to do it, but I'm sure I did the right thing.'

'And you think it was her?'

'One of them, one of the bodies, poor souls. Yes, there's a chance. A strong chance. She was a girl who took risks.' Mrs Marr sighed. 'And then there was her line. They'll be round asking questions about that, I suppose.'

'Uniforms, wasn't it?'

'That's right. There'll be talk.'

Mimsie nodded sagely, while repressing a grin. Who did Amelia think she was? There was always talk where she was, she lived on it, it was how she re-cruited custom.

'There was always a chance it was one of your girls.' No one knew better than Mimsie the dangers of life as Amelia Marr's girls lived it. And on the whole, they were the lucky, protected girls, looked after by Mrs Marr who was a canny one.

'Ex girl,' said Mrs Marr sharply. 'She'd left me, re-member. We've never had a death. Not on the prem-ises, anyway.'

One or two customers had been despatched in a hurry, but always breathing.

'You're in the clear,' said Mimsie soothingly. 'You did what was right according to your conscience, no one can say you didn't.'

'So I did,' agreed Amelia, although her conscience was an elastic one. She took comfort in her very strong local connections.

BECAUSE OF Mrs Marr's telephone call an identifica-tion of the first woman's body, that skeletal one, still wearing jeans and lying so close to the body of Peter Tiler, was made by her dentist.

She was Alice Mary Marchant, known profession-ally as Amy March.

The news was passed on to John Coffin by Inspector Archie Young, who had first informed Superintendent Paul Lane.

'Marchant or March was one of Mrs Marr's girls for two years. Very reliable, Mrs Marr says, whatever that means in the context. Then she said she was going back home to get married, although Mrs Marr didn't believe that, and left. There's a fair turnover of girls and she thought no more about it. Till today.'

'How long ago did March leave?'

'Mrs Marr was professionally vague. Said she couldn't really remember and she never kept records. Of course not, I said, but I bet she had a jolly good memory. She said she thought it was about eighteen months ago. The path people say March could have been dead about that long. The conditions where she was buried could have promoted rapid decomposition. Something to do with the soil.'

'What made Mrs Marr think one of the bodies could have been March?'

'Bit vague about that too, sir, but something to do with a mink wrap.'

'And the name, Amy March?' asked Coffin, mindful of his *Little Women*. 'Does that denote anything professionally?'

'No, sir, rather the reverse. It was a kind of in-house joke. Her speciality was uniforms. Yes, if you fancied a uniform, she was the girl you asked for.'

'Any uniform?'

'They had quite a collection.' He sounded admiring.

'Police included?'

'Yes, sir, I'm afraid so.'

'Does Marr think one of her customers did the job?'

'No, sir, she says all her customers are fully satisfied.'

'A lady with a sense of humour. She'll have to provide some names, all the same.'

'Oh yes, we'll get them out of her in the end.' If we don't know some of them already, Young thought, if rumour told the truth about one of his colleagues.

'It'll be a start,' said Coffin.

But he did not expect them to find the murderer from among Mrs Marr's clients. Somehow, it felt a stranger, wilder case than that.

He told Stella Pinero what he knew and he spoke to his sister Letty: he felt they had a right to know. And it was not as if it was going to be a secret for long. Mimsie Marker informed him of what she knew about Amy March as she handed him his evening newspaper on his way home, and what Mimsie knew, quite a number of other people soon knew as a rule. Mimsie played a vital role in the local communication network.

'She had a council flat over Leathergate way. Under her married name. Didn't like people knowing, but I knew.'

Of course you did, Mimsie, Coffin thought. 'So she was married?'

'Had been. Divorced, from what she said. Hamilton, that was the name. Talbot Buildings was where she had the flat. Still has, I expect. They don't care if you're alive or dead there.'

'In two years they'd notice, wouldn't they?'

'Wouldn't count on it. Why don't you take a look?'

Quietly, selfishly, Coffin went himself to Talbot Buildings, named after a local Labour MP, now dead, who had been a celebrated figure in early post-war Britain. Few people remembered him now, and almost certainly the inhabitants of Talbot Buildings knew not the man after whom their homes were named.

The estate, of which Talbot Buildings was but one block, had an estate manager and a social worker, with adjoining offices. Both of them were new to the job.

The estate manager, a bright young man, new from college and still keen on his job, consulted a list.

'Hamilton? No tenant of that name.'

'Not now,' said Coffin patiently. 'A year ago? You keep the records? Look back.'

'We could do with a computer here,' said the young man, obligingly pulling a card index towards him. 'Hamilton? Yes, here it is. Mrs H. A tenant for four years, always paid her rent on time, then cleared off, leaving a month owing.'

'So what did you do?'

'I wasn't here, but what I imagine happened was that after an interval we re-possessed her flat.'

'Weren't you worried, when she didn't come back?'

The estate manager raised a weary eyebrow.

'No, all right,' said Coffin, 'don't answer that. I suppose it happens all the time.'

'If you mean did we consult your lot, the answer is, I don't know, but if we did, then I doubt they did much. Not interested.'

No, thought Coffin, not until it is too late.

'So what did you do with her possessions? There were some, I take it?'

'See our social worker, Sue Armstrong. That's her, just going to her car. Grab her while you can, we don't see much of her round here, always on the wing.'

Sue Armstrong was a thin girl with a long, narrow, sceptical face, wearing the obligatory jeans and scruffy sweater.

She did not like policemen, very senior and distinguished policemen least of all.

'I hadn't been here long when Amy Hamilton left.'

'But you remember her?' He noticed her use of the Christian name.

She opened her car door. 'She must have had her reasons for going off. I don't feel it's my job to harry her.'

'You won't be doing that.'

She gave him a wary look. 'Why are you looking for her?'

He did not answer. Let her find out, as she would do. 'What happened to the things she left behind?'

'There wasn't much.' She was giving ground, perhaps becoming aware of the seriousness of his inquiry. 'They were put in store. My store. Eventually, I suppose, they will be sold or destroyed.'

'I'd like to see them.'

'All right. If you must. But they're hers, remember. Her property. Not just jumble.' She was being protective.

There was not much to see, just two plastic bags full. One contained clothes, the other a collection of small household goods. Among the electric kettle and the toaster was a small collection of paperback books. No letters.

Coffin picked up one of the books and from it fell a photograph. A snapshot of two women with the Thames and Tower Bridge in the background.

Sue looked at it. 'That's Amy. The one with curly hair. Pretty, wasn't she?'

'And the other girl?'

'Oh, that was her cousin from Newcastle. She came down to see the Royal Wedding. I don't think she ever came again.'

Coffin looked at the other girl, the visitor from the North. This girl was shorter than her cousin, a fatter, heavier figure, who had one foot in a built-up surgical boot.

'Oh, I think she did,' he said. 'I think she came again.'

What she did not manage to do was to leave.

HE WENT BACK FROM that interview to see if Stella was at home. She appeared at her door, in jeans and a white silk shirt with gold jewellery. Big spectacles were perched on her nose. 'I'm working,' she said unpromisingly. She was not pleased with John Coffin, not pleased at all. Once again, he had brought disturbing death into her life. He was going to ruin her production of *Hedda*. She wished she had never met John Coffin, but it was too late to worry over that now. As a matter of fact, she liked him very much, always had done and was getting to like him better every day. He knew it, too. Guessed it, responded to it. Her position was weak but potentially pleasurable. So her voice was not as cross as it might have been.

'I am going to make a telephone call, and then I want you to come with me to talk to Bridie.'

The telephone call was to Superintendent Paul Lane to acquaint him and DI Young with the fact that they now had the identity of a second murder victim, and that there was a close connection with Amy March, or Hamilton, late of Talbot Buildings, and that he thought a talk with Mimsie Marker might be productive. 'Sorry to throw you to the wolves, Mimsie,' he murmured to himself, 'but you undoubtedly know more than you are telling and probably always have done.'

He had picked up, with some amusement and without surprise because he had been expecting it, a slight irritation in the young Inspector's voice at the interference from The Old Man.

Stella was waiting for him outside her door. She had put a black velvet jacket over the silk shirt and removed her spectacles. A cloud of the scent of the season, Rose d'Automne, hung over her. 'I thought you'd forgotten what I told you.'

'I never forgot for a moment, but other things had to come first.'

'The story of my life,' said Stella, but without bitterness. 'I was making notes for the cast. My work, not yours. Not that I expect you to take it seriously.'

'I do, Stella, always have done. I take you seriously, too.' He looked at her fondly.

'Funny way of showing it.' But she was pleased.

'It's because I take you seriously that I want you to come with me to see Bridie. Will I find her at home?' Walking by her side and opening the door, he smelt the breath of roses. Would that reassure Bridie or alarm her? How did she feel about Stella Pinero?

Stella's answer reassured him. 'I think you will. I sent her home with instructions to rest. She looks a wreck, and gave a very poor rehearsal performance.' Stella's voice was kind and friendly: she was taking care of Bridie, their relationship was good, but she was in charge. 'Did I tell you your sister had got Peter Pond in as an angel? One with golden wings as far as I am concerned. He's laid on a hall for us to rehearse in. Draughty and not too clean, but private.'

'And how's it going?'

'Horrible at the moment, but I have hopes.' In fact, Stella knew she was building a good *Hedda Gabler*, full of vitality, and offering a Hedda whose motives were valid. She owed that to Lily Goldstone. She had a gem in the making, she could afford to be kind to Bridie.

When they arrived at Bridie's door, Stella took over.

'Hello, sweetie. You know this guy?'

Bridie gave him a nervous glance and nodded. Certainly she knew Coffin, she had been at the party in his flat. She also knew a rhetorical question when she heard one, knew what part they played in a piece of dramatic dialogue; they opened up a situation, accordingly she feared what was coming. Will appeared behind her, putting a controlling hand on her shoulder.

'Can we come in?'

Bridie looked at Will, but seemed to make the decision on her own account. 'Yes.' She stood aside. 'I've only got the one room,' she said. 'It's a bit untidy.'

Untidy was an understatement, Coffin felt, looking at the bed with the duvet falling off it and clothes on the floor, but Stella, used to the ways of her colleagues, accepted it easily. 'Just a talk, Bridie. No, don't go away, Will.'

'I wasn't.' His voice was hostile. Bridie stretched out a hand and took his. They looked more alive than ever, with the same deep-set blue eyes, the only difference being that Bridie's were red-rimmed as if she had been crying.

'Will has a room on the next floor,' said Bridie, as if she had to explain. Or wanted words to fill in the gap.

'I know,' Coffin said. Stella had told him. 'It's not Will I want to talk to but you.'

'Oh.' Bridie lowered her eyes and looked at the floor. 'Oh yes, I suppose that's because of Stella.' Her voice was hostile. 'I thought she'd tell you. But I don't really know anything about that pot.'

'Stella says she saw you carrying the urn. Or pot if you prefer. Why were you carrying it?'

'I don't know what it's all about,' said Bridie evasively. 'Sorry, Stella.'

'Oh, come on,' said Stella. 'It was you. You had it in your arms.'

Coffin sat down. No one had asked him to, but it made a point. He wasn't going away. He sat on the bed, there was nowhere else to sit, the only chair was piled high with books, scripts and clothes. 'I believe Stella. I'm going to press you on this. What were you doing and why did you do it?'

There was a long pause. Bridie did not look at Will, but Stella saw the girl toss back her hair and straighten her back. The gesture was familiar to Stella, who knew that Bridie was about to put on a performance.

'All right. I did see the urn. It was in the hall outside where you lived.'

'Oh.' He was surprised at that. So, if she was telling the truth, the urn had been placed outside his door. Really for him, then. 'You knew I lived there?'

'Of course, we all did.'

'So what did you do?'

'I'd seen it around the yard by the Workshop. I thought it was a prop and ought to go back. So I started to take it back. I suppose that's when Stella saw me.'

Coffin looked at Stella.

'Yes, that would be it.'

'And then?' Coffin looked at Stella.

'No more. That was it.'

'You didn't see the label on the urn?'

'No.'

'You didn't notice anything about the urn?'

'No.'

'It didn't feel heavier than you would have expected?'

'I didn't expect anything. I could see it was some sort of metal and not plastic, that's all. It was just a pot.'

'But you took the trouble to carry it back into the yard?'

'Theatre property, you see. There'd been an inventory and the ASM would be in trouble if it got lost. Pip's a friend of mine. We've been asked to be careful. Haven't we, Stella.'

Stella agreed that they had.

'So why deny you touched the urn?'

Bridie shrugged. 'I was frightened, I suppose. Frightened to admit I had touched it.' Her eyes were bright and wide, her voice calm. That's it, she was saying silently, and that's all I'm going to tell you.

'And did you, later, see anyone move the urn out into the street? Because someone did do that.'

'No,' said Bridie in a loud, clear voice, 'I did not see anyone do that.' There was conviction in her voice.

So telling and clear a conviction that Coffin immediately looked at Will. 'Did you?'

'No, I bloody well didn't,' said Will.

'It must have been a shock when the head was found in the urn?'

'Yes,' said Bridie. 'That's why I was upset. I've been telling you.'

Coffin stood up. The duvet slid to the floor, revealing a nightdress and a pair of tights. 'I'll see you again, both of you, and we'll continue this talk.'

As they left, Stella said: 'Well, you certainly stirred her anxieties up.'

'Yes, and I meant to.' He sounded exasperated. 'I'll get it out of her. Something there.'

When they were well away and the front door had closed behind them, Will said: 'What was all that about? I didn't know you'd touched the urn. Why did you do that?'

'Because I looked inside and saw Peter Tiler's head.'

'But why did you move it?'

'Because I thought you had killed Tiler.' She added, 'I was going to hide the pot. In the yard, somewhere. Then I dumped it in the street.'

'That was you.' It was a statement, not a question. 'What a lot you've kept from me, Bridie. I didn't kill

Peter Tiler. Why would I do anything as dreadful as that?'

'Because of what he said, because of what we did, because of what we are,' said Bridie.

JUST ABOUT the same time, Debbie Larger, who, with her husband Keith, was spending a few days in the country with their friends, the Frasers, made a worried comment to her husband.

'I've been trying and trying to get through to the flat, but no one answers. Karen ought to answer.'

But Karen was out looking for Billy, too scared to confess to her employers that she had betrayed their trust, not kept him safe, and that he had not been home. She was scouring the streets trying to find him.

'I don't know what to do,' Debbie said to her husband. 'I'm worried.'

'Get in touch with Ted Lupus and Kath,' he advised. 'Ask her to go round.'

'Yes, I'll do that.' She picked up the telephone again.

All this time, Little Billy was lying in his hiding-place, in a high fever, unconscious. He was having difficulty breathing. Deep inside him, he had the sensation that his legs were paralysed as the virus multiplied within him.

Katherine Lupus was contacted and said Yes, of course, she would be happy to help, she would like to find Billy.

ELEVEN

'I DON'T KNOW where the kid is,' said Stella. 'I didn't even know he was missing. I mean, it isn't as if I employ him. He just hangs around. Stage-struck.'

It was now late evening of that same day on which she had gone with John Coffin to speak to Bridie.

Stella had returned to her warm, quiet, haunted flat and made a pot of coffee. Since she was now in the middle of her weight-reducing diet, this had hit her stomach with force, giving her a minor high.

Back at work on her notes for the cast, she had been interrupted by a telephone call from Ted Lupus. It was her first intimation that the boy was missing and she was not, at first, inclined to take it seriously.

'No, I don't know where he is, Ted, he's a regular little street Arab and probably has any number of hideaways. You know what boys are like. Ask his schoolfriends. If you're really worried, you ought to tell the police.'

She went back to her work, not knowing what to make of this further mystery. Boys were boys, but on the other hand, nasty things had been happening around here. She found she wanted to tell someone, someone from her own dear theatre world who spoke her language, a worry shared, she thought; she reached out a hand for her telephone. 'JoJo?'

Little Billy had now been missing almost **twenty-four** hours.

THREE INTERLINKED circles had formed now and were in agitated motion.

There was the police circle in which moved John Coffin, Superintendent Paul Lane and Inspector Archie Young. This was the largest and the most varied circle. Within its circumference swung lesser circles made up of all those working on the multiple murder, such as pathologists and the different scientists, like chemists, physicists, and crystallographers, engaged in the various disciplines of forensic work. They now had the identities of two of the murdered women found in St Luke's, and were working towards the other two. Dr Wendy Nicholson, the epidemiologist, was part of this circle, whether she knew it or not, and even the sick Dr Schlauffer, now flown home to Germany to be nursed by his devoted wife. As yet, this group was not concerned with the missing boy, although they had learned of it, and anxiety was running through them.

Another circle was composed of Stella Pinero and the cast of *Hedda Gabler*. A flow of telephone calls was the method of communication here. They knew they would all be meeting in their rehearsal hall tomorrow (it very nearly was tomorrow) anyway. JoJo had answered her telephone promptly, Lily Goldstone had taken her time, and Charlie had only been reached by a message on his answering machine, but then everyone knew that Charlie kept his own hours. It was one of the things you turned a blind eye to, Stella knew that, and when he answered he was practical as always. 'The lad'll turn up. Take a pill and go to bed. I'm going to.'

The third and most frantic circle was made up of Kath and Ted Lupus, the Frasers and the anxious parents, Keith and Debbie Larger, who had come hurrying back from the Frasers' country estate. Even in her misery Debbie registered that the visit had been a success and that the Fraser house was definitely, to use an old phrase, now coming back into fashion, a place.

The circles touched and interlinked with each other, and were all, one way and another, in movement.

BY EARLY MORNING, all of this third circle was, with the exception of Katherine Lupus, in the sitting-room of the Largers' riverside flat. The Frasers and the Largers had driven up from the country before dawn. The au pair was weeping in a corner of the room, having received a lashing from Keith Larger's tongue of a ferocity that surprised everyone. But he blamed himself, this was his son, he loved him. Debbie also blamed herself. 'I'm the one really responsible,' she told them. 'What a rotten mother I have been. I can't even think of where he might have gone, of a place where he could be. That tells you something about me, doesn't it?'

Katherine Lupus was not present.

'Kath's out looking for Billy,' Ted Lupus explained. 'She seemed the best one, knowing youngsters the way she does. He'd trust her. I stayed here in your place ready to pass on any messages. And just in case Billy turned up.'

'What's been done so far?' Keith Larger was pacing up and down the room.

Agnes Fraser came quietly back into the room with a tray of coffee and toast. Even her youth and prettiness had drained away, but her kindness remained, showing as she went from person to person. They ought to try and eat, all of them. Ted Lupus took a cup of coffee and drank it thirstily, he had been up all night, in a state of considerable tension.

'Informed the police, of course. We did that first. Then Kath got in touch with all the local hospitals in case he'd been admitted. Your au pair—' here Ted glanced towards Karen—'thought he might have been unwell. But no news there. So then Kath got a list of all his schoolfriends from his teacher to find out if any of them knew anything.'

'Do they?'

'That's where she is now. Going round each address.'

'What about the theatre crowd?'

'I've called Stella Pinero. She didn't know anything. But she'll ask questions.'

'I see. Thanks, Ted. You and Kath have been very good.'

'Wanted to help.'

'No word from Kath?'

'She's out there looking.'

'That won't do much good if he's been murdered or kidnapped,' said Debbie with force.

'It's worth a try,' said Ted Lupus.

'You haven't got any children. You don't know how it feels.'

'Debbie,' protested Keith Larger.

'No, it's all right,' said Ted. 'I understand. No, I'm not a family man. Sadly. But I lost a young sister. I do know how it feels.'

Debbie put down the cup of coffee that Agnes had pressed on her. 'I'm going out too. I can't just sit here.'

'Eat something first.' Agnes was cutting a slice of toast into nursery fingers, as if that way they would be easier to eat. 'You had nothing yesterday, not to count. Try to eat some toast.'

Debbie shook her head.

'Better stay here,' said Ted Lupus heavily. He had his eye on Keith Larger, who got up.

'If anyone goes, it's going to be me.'

'Stay where you are, both of you.'

They sat there waiting.

ANOTHER PIECE OF LUCK came the way of Superintendent Lane, Inspector Archie Young and their team. They were in contact with all national police forces in their search for the identity of the two remaining women. Thameswater had all the bodies, but it was possible the women had come from outside the area. Already they knew that Beatie Fish, the cousin of Amy March or Hamilton, had come from Newcastle. They even knew now why she had not been reported missing.

Beatie was one of those people who have few kin and few contacts. She had had a job as a clerk in the Northern Maid Building Society in Newcastle, but when she left, saying she was going to visit her cousin in London and try her luck there, no one gave her another thought. Beatie hadn't even got a leaving present. Two of the girls took her out for a drink the night she left and then forgot her.

She was identified by the orthopædic surgeon who had operated on her left foot. 'Poor girl, poor girl,' he said. 'Yes, I recall those bones. The trouble was in the hip, of course, but the feet got distorted from the way she walked as a child.' He knew her foot even if he did not remember her face.

So they had a name for Beatie Fish who had come down to visit her cousin and been murdered with her, either at the same time or shortly afterwards. That was one piece of luck.

The other followed quite smartly and was, in a way, connected. Several pieces of Beatie's clothing had been sent for inspection to the laboratory in South London where Dr Marcia Glidding had a special expertise in fabrics. Fibres of every sort could speak with identifiable voices to her. As it turned out, Beatie's shirt and jeans, made of a mixture of cotton and synthetics, had come from a famous chain store and had nothing to offer of importance. But on the strength of what she had done, Dr Glidding was sent two plastic bags containing what was left of the clothes of the other victims.

She mused over threads drawn from the skirt and jacket of Victim Three, the tall lady. She had been wearing a suit of dark, thick woollen material, very hardwearing. Dr Glidding thought she could do something with those threads. They said something to her.

She had had the clothes of a hit-and-run victim sent to her for study some time before and the strands of cloth before her now reminded her of something. She got out her file on this case, which contained her report and specimen fibres neatly laid out.

She compared a fibre drawn from the skirt of Victim Three. They matched. They were uniform. They were from a uniform.

She picked up her telephone and asked to speak to Inspector Young, whom she knew slightly as a friend as well as a colleague. She knew his wife even better.

'Archie, this is just off the cuff, and I need to do some more work, but I wanted to give you a hint straight away. I think Victim Three may have been a traffic warden.'

Because she was a meticulous and sensitive worker, she had also picked out a thread of what had once been red cotton, the colour was still identifiable, that did not belong to the jacket or suit of Victim Three. It was alien thread, and as such, she carefully preserved it. Just in case.

This, although they did not know it, was very fortunate for the combined Lane-Young investigating team.

But the real piece of luck, and this, too, lay in the future, was that Marcia Glidding knew Archie Young's wife and that she would shortly be meeting her at a dinner.

John Coffin was going to be at that dinner, too. In fact, he was to be one speaker and Dr Glidding the other.

With the added assistance of Dr Glidding's interesting suggestion, the police were able to pick out Victim Three from their list of missing women who were of the right height and age. There were only three, and only one, Josephine Hudson of Tunnel Walk, Greenwich, was a Traffic Warden. She had been missing for three years.

Josephine, Mrs Hudson, had last been seen walking toward the entrance of the tunnel under the Thames which led from Greenwich to the Isle of Dogs.

Her husband had reported her missing, but since they were on bad terms following a violent quarrel about her behaviour, he had come under some suspicion of having done away with her, and after an initial period of being willing to talk freely, had refused to answer any more questions. Nothing could ever be proved against him. The file on Josephine was still open, but no progress had been made.

'I remember it all well,' said the local Inspector with whom Young was speaking. 'It was a real bugger. She just seemed to disappear into thin air. I thought it was the husband, I must say.'

'Any evidence?'

'None. There was a lot of building going on across the river just then. I must say I always had the idea that Hudson popped his wife in a hole where the Dockland Railways was going on the Dogs, and that was why we couldn't find her. I thought he did it.'

'We may find he did.'

'He won't do you any good, he's dead. Topped himself two years ago. So maybe it was him and he had a guilty conscience.'

Young duly reported his progress to his Superintendent, who said it was good as far as it went, which wasn't far, but that anyway things had started to move, and reminded him to tell the Chief Commander.

It was well into that morning when people were still looking for Little Billy when John Coffin was told on the telephone.

'Good, good.' He found the details fascinating. 'Was she going out to work? Or did she wear her uniform all the time?'

'That seems to be it, sir. She loved her uniform, wore it as often as she could. Tried to join the Force, it seems, but she couldn't make the grade. The uniform was one of the things that irritated her husband. That and her wandering ways. She was inclined to pick up men in pubs and go off to the park with them.'

'Ah.'

'Yes. It does kind of slot her in with the other victims. Explains how the murderer got on terms with them.'

'One killer for all the women, then?'

'That's how it looks. We're not looking for more than one at the moment. The pattern for all the women is so strong and consistent. Don't you agree, sir?'

'Yes, I do.'

'It says something about the murderer, too. He looked out for the sort of women who took risks.'

'I agree.'

'There is something else too, sir. He may have been keen on women in uniform. Mrs Marr has admitted that Amy March's speciality was uniforms.'

Coffin remembered what Stella had told him about the actress, Rosie Ascot: Rosie had played the part of a policewoman in the TV series. She too had a background with a uniform in it.

'Ascot fits into that slot,' he said. 'A consistent chap, this killer.'

'And with peculiar tastes. That ought to help.'

'I doubt if he's got it written all over him, but yes, it settles his sex.'

'Sex ambivalent, I'd say, sir,' said Archie alertly.

Coffin laughed. 'Think he dresses up in high heels?'

'Well, he could.'

'It's an idea. We'll look for a man with small feet.'

'Big hands, a strong man, all these women were overpowered and strangled. Not gassed, as with Christie.'

'If I had to guess, I'd say he was an unassuming sort of man, one they trusted, an apparently nice chap.'

They were half joking, the sentences batted back and forth between them lightly, but both knew there was serious intent there as well.

They were beginning to put forward a profile of this murderer: a man who appeared unassuming, but who was physically stronger than he may have looked. A man attracted to women of power. A wily, cunning man, able to assume a mask.

'What about Mrs Tiler? Does she fit into that pattern?'

'She has to, somehow,' said Coffin thoughtfully. 'We need to find out more about her.'

'And then there's Tiler. Was he killed because his wife was killed?'

Peter Tiler was the joker in the pack, head and all.

'There's more than a hint he was a blackmailer. He may have been killed because of that.'

'You'll have all the reports in detail,' said Archie Young briskly, feeling he had done his bit. Offered information freely to the Old Man, accepted comment in return, shared a joke. Now he'd done, and back to work.

One more thing.

'You've heard about the boy, sir? The Larger boy is missing.'

'No, I hadn't heard.' Coffin was on the alert at once. 'Any reason to believe it's connected with the case?'

'No evidence that way at the moment. But . . .'

But when you had a case of such extreme nastiness, then you had to take on board anything odd that happened in the neighbourhood. There might be a connection.

'There's a search on, usual places. Parks, railway cuttings, building sites.'

'Plenty of them.'

'As you say, sir. But no sign yet.'

'I've met the lad. I hope you find him soon.'

Coffin went off to the last meeting of his day, one with the Home Office representative about the services in his area.

He felt he handled the interview well, protecting the interests of his new Force without being tactless. I'll make a politician yet, he thought.

But underneath ran the current of his concern with the murders. There was something they were not quite getting.

The urn. What about the urn with Peter Tiler's head in it? From the killer's point of view that action had to be justified.

Know that, he thought to himself, and we'll know everything.

He was WALKER again that evening. Taking the Dockland Railway as far as it would go, studying this new River City, not yet a city but an imaginative leap, which his struggling Force might help bring to birth. A heavily populated area, old buildings jostled by new ones, a network of new streets followed ancient paths.

The odd decayed, unreconstructed lot still holding its secrets. More than a few people could lie hidden in this city without discovery. He didn't give Little Billy much of a chance if he didn't turn up soon.

Through Shadwell, Limehouse, Leathergate (where you could change to the Tube), Heron Quays, South Quay, Mudchute, and then getting out at the station called Island Gardens and walking through the tunnel where Josephine Hudson had last been sighted.

The subway under the Thames was a late Victorian piece of engineering, solid and determined, its character unchanged since the day it was opened in 1902, the clinical white tiling and thick ironwork denoting that it was meant for the use of a working-class population to use to go about its labours. The tunnel's æsthetics had now found their period and in the 1980s it was a cult object. Tourists came to see it.

He walked through to the other side, looked around at an area where he had once worked and lived, then turned back. His writ did not run here.

WALKER IS BACK ACROSS the river, and heading homewards, came the relieved report. They hated him to be out and on the loose, his circle vibrating to his own particular movements.

IT WAS STILL POSSIBLE to deliver coffee and sandwiches from Max's delicatessen to the hall where the cast of *Hedda Gabler* were meeting, so Stella had ordered and Max had duly sent round a tray, carried by one of his daughters. This one was known to the cast as 'The Fat Daughter', although they were all plump, but it distinguished her from another daughter who was not thin but was extremely handsome. They called her 'The Beauty'. There was also a third daughter who was known as 'The Little One', she was the youngest and smallest and fattest. All three girls had been down with the virus of unknown origin which so interested Dr Wendy Nicholson, but had recovered easily. JoJo Bell was still complaining of odd weaknesses, but Dr Nicholson had pronounced in a TV interview that adults suffered a worse infection and recovered more slowly than children so JoJo said she knew what she was in for. A relapse any day might be expected and how was Bridie, she looked peaky? In for it too, no doubt.

Stella kept silent on what she knew or did not know about Bridie and her troubles. JoJo was consulting the Equity rules, while Lily Goldstone read a contract sent to her by her agent.

She stretched out a hand. 'Lend me the book of rules, Jo. I want to check this contract.'

'I can do that for you.'

'I'm better at it myself.' Better at it than anyone. No one could beat Lily Goldstone at bending the rules. Not necessarily to her own advantage, but to what she considered a kind of natural justice. She was naturally litigious. Lily in the Middle Ages, Lily as an abbess, would have been a formidable lady, always ready to defend the rights, privileges and territory of the foundation. In many ways she had missed her period.

Charlie Driscoll, cup in hand, wandered across to JoJo and muttered a query.

Big spectacles on her nose, hair tied back in a pony tail, still looking pale, but in excellent spirits, JoJo said: 'From what I can gather, the police think now that Peter Tiler was killed by the murderer of all those poor women. Probably tried blackmail. So you are in the clear, Charlie. We all are.'

'You think so?' Charlie sounded far from sure.

'Well, naturally the police are not telling me everything, but I have a certain position as Equity rep—' JoJo looked important—'so I have been able to ask questions and get answers.'

Lily raised her head from her researches. 'Take no notice of JoJo. She has no judgement.'

'As good as yours any day.'

'If it was, you'd be a better actress.'

'We don't all take our standards from Shaftesbury Avenue,' said JoJo loftily.

'Oh, shut up, you two,' said Charlie.

Bridie, who had given a good, even moving, performance which Stella prayed would be repeated (something you could never rely on with novice performers, especially those in love), was sitting hunched in a corner. She saw Stella approaching her, cup in hands, and she stood up.

'Hello, Bridie, how are you feeling this morning?'

'Much better, Stella.' She was pale, but calm.

'You were all right today. Pretty good, in fact.' Stella was never lavish with her praise, but this seemed an occasion to say something nice. 'Just one or two points. I'll give you a note.'

'Thank you.' Bridie took a deep breath. 'I was coming to speak to you, Stella.'

'Go ahead.'

'I'm going to give all this up. Acting, I mean. I'm going into an order. Take a vow. I'm going to be a nun.'

Stella opened her mouth, then closed it again.

'I'm sorry if it's a shock,' said Bridie gently. 'It's not so surprising as you might think. Or as sudden. I always had it in my mind. We're Catholics, you know, in my family.'

'Oh Bridie, what will they think about it?'

'Oh, they won't mind. It's what my mother always wanted for me.'

'Sit down, Bridie.' Stella found a chair for herself and sat down too. 'We must talk about this. Have you discussed it with anyone?'

'It's my decision.' It was Bridie at her gentlest and most implacable.

'You have the makings of a very good actress, Bridie. Perhaps more than that. I would risk saying you could be exceptional. I don't like the waste of such a gift. Such a rare gift.'

'No gift is ever wasted.'

'That depends. There's something behind this, isn't there? You know, you are very gifted. In a different class from, say, Will. He has the looks and the sexual appeal.'

'Oh, he has that all right,' said Bridie bitterly.

There was a pause.

'Where is Will?'

'I don't know. Around. He said he didn't want any coffee.'

'Have you two had a row?'

'No.'

Stella stood up. 'Think about it, Bridie, and think again. I don't believe nature intended you to be a nun.'

Stella met Will by the table, just reaching for a sandwich.

'All right, Will?'

'Been out to get a breath of air.'

'Probably a good idea.'

'How did it go today?'

'You were fine, Will, just fine. You need to relax a little.'

'I could do with a strong drink.'

'Not at work.'

'But we all do, sometimes. I've heard of some great actors who perform better when drunk.'

'Not you, Will,' said Stella with sincerity. 'Not you. You're far too young for that game, and not yet great. And you never will be if you carry on that way. All you'll get will be the sack. I shall see you never work again.' A threat she would not carry out, but which might make him think.

As she moved away, Will said: 'Any news about the boy?'

Silently, Stella shook her head. No news. No news was not, in matters of this sort, good news.

From where she sat, JoJo called out: 'I heard that Kath Lupus was out doing her bit.'

Stella sipped her coffee, a faint twang sounded inside her as she felt the vibration of the circle of which she was a part.

KATH LUPUS had gone back to her own home for a wash and a change of clothes, after a night spent looking for Little Billy in company with the Largers' au pair who had been less than no help, but anyway someone to walk with. This wasn't an area where you wanted to be absolutely on your own at night, not even if you are Kath Lupus, who fears nothing. Or almost nothing.

She was going out again when she had finished her coffee and toast. This time taking with her a young policewoman.

Kath had earlier extracted a list of Billy's friends from the headmistress of the drama school where he had been a pupil for two years. The headmistress, roused from her sleep, had consulted her files and class lists and given Kath the name of Little Billy's class teacher. This lady supplied names and addresses. All this had taken Katherine some time when she felt the need for haste. She could really have done without a police escort but she had not been in a position to refuse.

Katherine Lupus and WPC Grey set out on their tour.

John Coffin, driving in his official car to one of his planning committees in the City (in his mind it was already 'the old City'), saw them at the corner of Pavlov Street at the beginning of this progression. He had been informed of Kath Lupus's helping hand. If anyone knew the district she ought to, and she knew the boy as well.

BILLY, IT BECAME CLEAR, did not have many friends, not because he was an unfriendly boy but because his energies were directed towards the Theatre Workshop. He was in some ways advanced for his age, a sophisticated lad, in other ways a kind of throwback. He would have enjoyed an apprenticeship in old-fashioned rep, fitted in perfectly with the Crummles and might well have felt at home walking on for Will

Shakespeare. That's the sort of lad who created Juliet, Stella had once thought, summing him up perceptively.

Kath and her travelling companion came to the first address, with the policewoman driving. Folly Fitzgerald, a chubby child with a toss of auburn curls whose agent (and mother) always described her in her publicity handouts as a Moppet, opened her wide, worldly eyes to explain that Yes, she was a pal of Billy but she hadn't seen much of him lately. He was so in with the Theatre Workshop crowd, while she had been so busy doing a TV commercial for Betty Bloomer Kiddy Clothes. She raised a weary eyebrow. Dreadful style but they did pay well.

Exit Folly Fitzgerald.

Kath Lupus and WPC Grey left the neat bungalow named Tara which seemed totally devoted to Folly and her work, and passed on to a large run-down house with no name and a barely legible number where lived John and Jolly Benson, identical twins whose value to Billy as friends must have been purely on their curiosity value, since they had nothing much to say to the outside world, communicating only with each other.

They listened to questions, though, with the keen interest of those to whom the scene outside themselves is an alien world. Nature had constructed them to be perpetual foreigners who needed to learn the routes.

Acting as guide, Kath Lupus introduced the subject of Billy Larger. The twins were polite boys and did their best to show her their world too. They were dancers, they said, and not into straight theatre, so they hadn't known Billy very well, but they had gone around together for a while because he was such a good talker. That was a help to them, they implied.

But they hadn't seen him lately and didn't know where he could be now. One spoke and the other echoed. There always had to be a front man and they had silently elected the Elder Twin. Tomorrow the younger one might have a go, trying the part on for size to see how it fitted him.

They saw their visitors to the door, holding hands and moving in unison, little feet tapping a neat pattern.

Kath and WPC Grey crept away from those dancing feet. One more friend to visit. This time an adolescent boy, whose parents were both actors, and who spared a few minutes before going off to a singing lesson to explain that Billy was a real pro but needed to groom up his act a bit. But give him time, give him time, and he'd be great, great.

No, he had no idea where Billy was, their contacts had been entirely professional, Billy liked talking to both his parents about stagecraft, if they'd talk about it, which his mother would and mostly the Guvnor wouldn't, and had been even keener since his father took over as Director of the Havisham Festival. So had quite a few other kids. He, Roger, had never had any illusions, and if they would now excuse him . . . ?

They did, and collapsed into Max's for a cup of coffee.

'Any news of the boy?' Max brought their coffee himself. He knew what they had been doing. If Mimsie Marker was one centre for gossip and information, then Max's delicatessen was certainly another.

He nodded politely to WPC Grey. Always keep in with the police.

'Not yet.' Kath took a reviving sip of hot coffee. 'Hopeful.'

'I saw Mr Larger go by.' Max knew everyone. Anyway, Deborah Larger was one of his best customers. Even bought the best Beluga to go on a cheese mousse she made. 'I suppose he's out looking too.'

'Couldn't do anything else,' said Kath. 'Don't suppose he can rest.'

'I'd be the same if it was one of mine.'

'How are yours?' asked Kath, who thought she had seen the flash of a cotton skirt round the door to the kitchen. Shouldn't that girl be at school?

'Over what they had, whatever it was. Some virus. But I'm keeping Clara at home. She helps her mother, who is not so well.'

Kath gave an involuntary frown. The headmistress in her did not approve of that.

'How are you, Mrs Lupus?' asked Max. 'You don't look so good yourself.'

'Bit of a headache. It's the strain. Nothing. If only we could find the boy. I think he's hidden somewhere. There must be someone who knows where he might have put himself.'

Or been put. But she dared not say that aloud.

Clara, who had been listening from the kitchen while she polished glasses, pursed her lips. Then, because she was a discreet and circumspect girl, she went to consult her mother.

Kath Lupus and WPC Grey were about to leave when Clara appeared at the back of the shop. She was carrying a couple of warm scented towels in a bowl.

'Mother thought you might like a tidy up if you've been on the go all the morning.'

'Oh, that's kind.'

'I'll show you the way. There's a nice big mirror.'

Max had been very careful to meet all hygiene regulations when fitting out his new shop, so that the little washroom was sparkling and bright. Kath washed her hands and face and applied new lipstick. One of those days, she thought, when you look worse with lipstick on than off.

The girl hovered in the background, straight-faced. Presently, Kath Lupus's extra sense, derived from years as a headmistress, alerted her to the fact that the girl had something to communicate. A glance at WPC Grey told her that the policewoman had noticed too.

Kath knew it was up to her to start. The girl wanted to speak, but she needed a push. 'How's your mother, Clara?'

'Getting better, thank you, Mrs Lupus.'

'And how are you? I know you've been ill.' Clara was a nice girl, but slow, all her teachers said so. You had to give her time, she wouldn't hurry herself.

'I'm well now, thank you, Mrs Lupus.'

'Back to school soon?'

'I hope so.'

'Is there anything you wanted to say?'

Clara nodded. 'It's about Billy. He comes in here for a Coke sometimes. We talk, you know?' Kath nodded. 'I know he's missing, and I think I might know where he is.'

Clara elaborated on her theme.

'DO YOU THINK she knew what she was talking about?' asked WPC Grey, as they walked away.

'I think she did. It sounded right. Billy was the sort of boy to have a hideout. Boys do that sort of thing.'

'But would he tell her?'

'Yes, I think so.'

'She's quite pretty. A bit overweight, but nice.'

'Yes, she is.'

And, somehow, motherly for her age and size. Kath recognized that a boy like Billy, somewhat short of maternal love, might confide in Clara. She wondered exactly what he had said. More perhaps than Clara had let on. Other secrets, other confessions?

'But she didn't know exactly where this place might be, so where are we going?' asked WPC Grey. She asked politely, because she was always polite and had been told to accompany and help Mrs Lupus, a respected local figure, but she did want to know where Kath was so confidently leading her now. 'Do we take the car?'

'Not now. We'll do better on foot.'

'But where?' WPC Grey stuck to her point. She was not moving a foot without some information.

'Clara didn't know the name of the street, but she gave a pretty accurate description of where it was and what it looked like.' Katherine Lupus lived in the neighbourhood, she had worked in it for years, and her husband's building firm had helped to knock down a lot of the old landscape and to construct the new one. She carried a picture of the district in her head, and she knew where she was going. 'Not far from the river, the remains of a workman's hut, but hidden by a street of new houses. In a cul-de-sac.'

There was such a place, Kath wondered why she hadn't thought of it before.

'She didn't say that.'

'She doesn't know the phrase. A kind of little alleyway, she called it.' But Kath knew the area, and she had knowledge that WPC Grey and the police did not have. 'Also, remember it has to be within walking distance of the Theatre Workshop.' Or running distance. The boy had run.

'Does it? Why?'

'Because the boy was on his way home, and he never got there.'

'I don't think it quite follows. But I get what you mean. So where are we going?'

'Nearly there.'

Not many yards from St Luke's and the Theatre Workshop, a building which had formed a part of the old docks had been converted into several expensive flats. The former yard of the building now contained a square of rather charming mews-type houses. These had only just been completed (not by Ted Lupus's firm but by a competitor, but which Kath knew about) and now stood empty.

The old gatehouse stood between the flats and the mews houses. It had been used as the site manager's office while building work was going on but was on the point of being renovated into a period town house. A handsome building, it had its own narrow back yard, now filled with builder's debris and rubbish.

This yard was nothing more than a passageway designed to give entrance to the back of the house. Kath remembered noticing it when she had gone with a friend to view one of the mews houses, which the friend had bought. To her mind, it exactly fitted the description Clara had given them of where Billy might be.

'It's worth a look here,' she said, halting WPC Grey at the gate. 'Just in case.' Inside herself, she was sure the boy was here, somewhere.

'In the house?' The girl looked up at the building, empty and boarded up.

'No. In the yard.'

There was a side passage to the yard through which the two of them pushed, elbowing their way through the general rubbish. A grating in the floor gave light to some subterranean hole.

The little yard was empty except for more rubbish. But at the side two steps led down to what must have been a coal cellar once. The grid in the passage was probably where it got its light.

You could stand underneath there, Kath thought, and see into the street. A boy would like that. Workmen on the site might certainly have created a cosy hideaway for themselves. It fitted Clara's description of what the boy had told her.

'Let's have a look down here,' she said, leading the way down the steps. 'Mind how you go.'

There was a sign of human habitation, a bit of carpet, an old armchair. There was the smell of humanity, not a good smell.

In the light from the grating, Kath saw a figure curled up on the floor, lying on a pile of newspapers.

She turned to the girl behind her. 'We've found him. Get help.'

'How is he? Is he dead?'

Kath knelt down by the boy.

'No, I don't think so. Alive, but unconscious.'

Little Billy, who had experienced a range of symptoms, many of which had been enjoyed by other victims of the virus who had felt breathless, semi-paralysed and full of pain, heard her voice yet kept his eyes firmly closed.

TWELVE

LITTLE BILLY lay safely in hospital, and he meant to stay there. He was putting on the act of his life.

The medical staff were puzzled at his condition. They believed he had had a bad case of the virus which had afflicted so many people, he still had a high temperature, it was possible he had a residual weakness in his legs, they could not be sure, but he should be responding to their calls for wakefulness, and he was not.

'We don't know what to make of it,' said the young male houseman into whose nervous care Billy had been entrusted. Dr Blood (he came from a long line of local doctors) had only qualified three months ago, this was his registration year, he didn't want anything to go wrong. 'But he isn't speaking and light seems to worry him. He doesn't open his eyes.' He had caught a flicker from the patient's eyes once or twice, and the night sister could have told him about a long hard stare round the darkened ward in the small hours, but she kept information like that for the consultant or at the very least the senior registrars. With every minute that passed she was becoming increasingly sceptical about Billy's responses.

'You don't think he has brain damage?' whispered his mother. Debbie Larger was sitting by the bed, her hand tightly gripping Billy's.

Dr Blood looked alarmed. 'It's too early to tell.' His patient both interested and puzzled him. He had experienced a strong desire to stick a pin in the boy to see if he jumped, but he recognized this as an ignoble impulse. Billy might be putting it on a bit, but why?

Billy was lying there with a chart at the foot of his bed listing all his vital functions, his temperature which was now approaching normal, his blood pressure and some more technical details about his bowels, bladder, and body fluids. He shouldn't have been unconscious, but it seemed he was.

'How are you feeding him?' Keith Larger got down to basic facts.

'He responds to spoonfuls of food, so he can swallow. And we've got him on a drip.'

Little Billy's stomach gave a convulsive twitch. After a period of pain and nausea, it now cried out for hamburgers and chips, fried back bacon and hot toast, with chocolate ice-cream to follow. It was not happy with the pap it was getting.

'I noticed the drip,' said Keith Larger. 'Wondered if it was necessary.'

Little Billy was listening, but with detachment. Let them get on with it, he was not going to utter. Then, because he was comfortable after what truly had been a very gruelling time, he began to drift off to sleep.

Thoughts idly drifted through his mind. He had hidden because he believed the murderer was after him, had seen feet that alarmed him. Then he had become very ill, that part was misty and vague. Now he was in hospital and the murderer was still after him. He had reason to believe so. He was better off where he was.

His mother's hand felt comforting rather than otherwise. She could stay, but no other visitors were allowed. They appeared to distress the patient. Billy was rather proud of the way he appeared able to send up his pulse and blood pressure when anyone came near his bed. He didn't know how he did it but he thought it showed he was a real trouper.

On the other hand, it might be genuine fear.

As BILLY LARGER deliberately lost his voice, so the murderer of Peter Tiler increasingly found his. It rumbled away inside the murderer in a gravelly, neutral kind of voice, internal voices being sexless, demanding confession.

It was a judgemental killing, it said, you will be praised for it.

Naturally the killer did not altogether believe this, internal voices being frequently wrong, because they are after satisfaction, not prophecy.

Not being heeded, it continued its communication in another way, seeping into the atmosphere by a kind of osmosis, causing pains, headaches and irritations all round.

You shall know me by my behaviour, it was saying, even if not by my words.

Little Billy was a known and recognized invalid, but he was safely tucked up in his hospital bed, where his parents felt he could be left for the time being; they went home to get some rest. Debbie ached from head to foot, and Keith felt his ulcer playing up. The au pair having tactfully absented herself (she was doing her packing with a view to going home), Debbie and Keith went to bed.

The Frasers gratefully faded into their own lives again, once Billy was located, taking with them as their share of infected anxiety an attack of migraine for the Lord Mayor, who nevertheless had to be host at a City dinner next day, and the sudden fear of his wife that all her hair was falling out. There certainly seemed to be a lot of it about, on her shoulders, on her pillow and even in the Lord Mayoral car. 'I feel like a dog that is moulting,' she said.

Ted and Kath Lupus followed them home, Kath with one of the raging headaches that were going the rounds and Ted sunk in a misery so extreme that he could not speak.

They drove past St Luke's with its church, now a domestic dwelling, and its hall, now the Theatre Workshop, and he wished he had never seen it or that it would burn down, in spite of the fact that it was a profitable contract and his men were still at work there. As far as the police would allow them to be.

'All those poor women buried there,' he said, as he changed gears and headed for Pavlov Street. 'If only I'd known.'

'What would you have done?'

'Blown the bloody place up. What would you have done?'

Kath kept silent. She had a sudden vision of dead limbs being blasted into the air, scattering legs and arms on the traffic thundering past to central London, and distributing bits and pieces all over Leathergate and Spinnergate. They would probably not reach as far as Swinehouse and Easthythe.

'Thank God it's half term,' she said aloud. 'And I need not see another child for a week. Except Billy. I'll visit him.'

'He's not allowed visitors,' said Ted as he parked the car. 'His father said so.'

'I must not let that apply to me,' said his wife. 'Are there any aspirin? I must have a painkiller.'

'LIFE'S A BUGGER,' said Charlie Driscoll, summing it up for himself and more than one of the others. He went home to pace his living-room and feel miserable. Life was pinching him in places where he felt he did not deserve it.

Rehearsals had been aborted that day for the cast of *Hedda Gabler*, sickness and bad temper had taken over here, too. Stella Pinero, not usually one to let up on the discipline of regular work, recognized that with one member of the cast hieing away to a nunnery, another taking to drink, and yet another, Lily, on the point of a lawsuit with both her agent and the producer of her latest film, it was time to relax the rules. The Equity rep had advised it, and for once Stella was taking her advice.

One by one, the cast melted away to their own preoccupations. They had heard about Little Billy's rescue, which was a relief, but their spirits were not greatly raised. Who was going to come to their show, when the excitements of the world outside were so real? Ibsen was competing with multiple murder and raging sickness and not going to win.

Stella took JoJo and Lily Goldstone off for coffee at Max's. These two were her main allies in the company. When it came down to it, she preferred working with women, whom she found more reliable than men.

'I suppose you've heard about Bridie's nonsense?' she asked. 'Coffee for us all, Max, and a ham croissant for me.' Dieting be damned, her stomach raged for solid food.

They agreed that they had heard, but it might not be nonsense, there was a desperate look about Bridie.

'Poor Will, look what it's doing to him. Drink. That's no answer. All he needs is straight sex to set him right. I might have to take him on myself and make him over,' said Lily, who had long fancied Will.

'The girl thinks she's sinned,' said Stella, biting into her croissant.

'Oh God, I do detest and despise the Anglo-Saxon sense of sin,' cried Lily viciously, in her best National Theatre voice, causing a customer at another table to look round nervously.

'Never worried you, dear,' said JoJo. 'But then you're not really Anglo Saxon, are you? I think I'll have one of those croissants. I know they're junk food, but I feel the need to bite into something soft and warm.'

'That's not a bad bit of dialogue,' said Lily appreciatively. 'You know, Jo, your future might be in writing more than acting.'

'Oh, do you think so? I've often thought so myself.'

They settled into a companionable discussion.

Stella drank her coffee while continuing to worry about Bridie. 'You don't think, do you, that Bridie's behaviour has anything to do with the murders?'

'Yes, a bit,' said JoJo. 'We're all a bit touched by it.'

'Bridie never killed all those women,' declared Lily bluntly.

'Never said so. But there might be more than one murderer about,' said JoJo.

'You can be so cheerful,' said Stella, putting down her croissant.

JoJo shrugged. 'She might suspect Will. We're all looking at each other sideways, aren't we? I know I am.'

'Thank you.'

'Oh, not you especially, Stella. I've known you for years. But I don't know Will, although he's lovely to look at, and Charlie's a queer cuss.'

'I've known Charlie for years,' said Stella, in a weak voice.

'Ah, but have you? Think about it,' said JoJo, wagging her finger. 'And then there's poor Mrs Tiler, everyone seems to have forgotten about her, but she was killed too.'

'Did you know her?' asked Stella. 'You grew up round here.'

'No,' said JoJo shortly, 'I was just making a point.'

'Open your mouth to the police round here and they'll hang you,' said Lily.

'That's not fair on the police,' protested Stella.

'If you happen to have been born here, or have family, then watch it, that's my advice.'

Stella finished her coffee, paid her bill and prepared to depart before they quarrelled. 'I'm going to get a paper. My copy of *The Stage* hasn't come this week. I don't know where I'll get one this late.'

All of them relied on their weekly newspaper for the gossip of their craft.

'I've heard they're looking for a new Director at Chichester.'

'Not again,' said JoJo.

'Not that I'd apply, of course.'

'Of course not,' said JoJo loyally.

But a discreet word in the right ear, and one might be asked to put oneself forward.

'So I want to see if it's mentioned.' Stella moved towards the door.

'Pippa Barnes is leaving *Sunlight and Starshine*,' announced JoJo suddenly. 'Best job she's had in years. Leaving. Saw that in *The Stage*. Didn't see the Chichester thing.'

'Why's she leaving?' asked Lily.

'Ill health, it said. Drink, more like it. She threw a wine bottle at the conductor. You won't find that in *The Stage*.'

'All the same, I must get a copy.'

'Try Mimsie.'

'Go to Mimsie,' called Stella. 'She'll give you all the dirt.'

International, national and local.

MIMSIE PRODUCED a copy of *The Stage*, slightly crumpled as if she had read it herself first. But she made no charge, which Stella thought was fair, so she bought several copies of expensive and glossy magazines (one bearing a large portrait of a rival actress on the cover, which instantly she promised herself to deface) to level things up.

She did not have to introduce the subject of Bridie, because Mimsie started on it herself.

'So you're losing one of your youngsters?'

'How do you know?'

'Her mother told me. She's all over the place. After asking God to fix it for her for years, now she's upset that he has.'

'The girl seems to feel she has to work out some sin,' said Stella gloomily. 'I think there's a kind of sickness round here at the moment and it's taking people different ways. This is her share.'

Mimsie cackled. 'If there's a sin, it's further back in the family.'

'What do you mean?'

'Oh, I can tell you what's worrying her. If you knew more about the neighbourhood, you'd know yourself. Or if you had eyes in your head.'

Stella stared at her dumbly.

'She's not pregnant, is she?' she asked after a bit.

'Not that I know of, although she may be. No, haven't you looked at her and young Will together?'

'Well,' began Stella, 'I suppose I have...'

'And don't they look alike?'

'They do, now you mention it. But you don't mean...?' She paused.

'Same father. That's the story, but I doubt it myself. Bridie's mother would have told me. No, someone got a bit mixed up somewhere, I don't doubt, but not that generation.'

'Poor young things,' said Stella, thinking that even if it wasn't true, they believed it, especially if they'd been to bed together.

'Personally, I'd tell them to forget it and get on with it.'

'You're a pagan, Mimsie.'

'No, I'm not, I'm natural. Look at cats and doggies. My old Timmy mated with his sister and they had lovely little kittens. Seven of them, as healthy as could be.'

'What did you do with them, Mimsie?' asked Stella absently, folding up *The Stage* and still thinking about Bridie and Will.

'Found them all good homes. I had him neutered afterwards, though, just to be on the safe side. We can't have too much of a good thing, can we?'

Incest, thought Stella, all right for cats, but you didn't really want it in the family. Supposing Bridie and Will were suddenly confronted with the tale by Peter Tiler, together with a threat of blackmail?

No, it was not good news for anyone who wanted to think Will innocent of murder.

When Stella had heard of the several bodies found in the crypt of St Luke's, their deaths spread over a period of years, she had felt relief. This lets us out, she had thought. Now, however, it looked as though one of the deaths could be back as a personal problem.

But the head in the urn? Would Will do that? And if so, why? She found she could not believe in gentle, restrained (and oh so good-looking) Will chopping off Peter Tiler's head and putting it in a pot.

Hands too, she told herself with a shudder, don't forget the hands.

She left Mimsie's stall, tucking *The Stage* under her arm. 'Mimsie? If I live all through this, and sometimes, I think I won't, a kind of feeling, you know, Mimsie, then can I have one of your kittens, if there's one around?'

It would be nice to have a cat to come home to.

ON THE WAY HOME she decided to buy some food in Max's delicatessen. She did not want to eat Chinese, or Indian, or any other of the ethnic variations available to her locally. She wanted to have a tray of food on her lap and watch something trivial on the television.

The shop was crowded when she got there so that she had to wait her turn, during which time she occupied herself reading *The Stage*. The copy provided by Mimsie had stains on it as if Mimsie had been drinking while she read. The smell that floated up to Stella in the warmth of the shop was delicately beery.

She gradually became aware of a familiar voice in the queue in front of her, saw a tall back, broad shoulders and a still thick head of hair, growing grey in a suitably distinguished way, and heard her friend, John Coffin, asking in diffident voice for ham cut thin, but not too thin.

As he passed her on the way out, bearing his parcel of ham and a long baton of bread, she breathed to him to wait for her and they could walk home together. He nodded, his face tired.

I could look after that man, thought Stella, but perhaps I shouldn't bother.

People didn't always want it, were not always grateful. As why should they be, when it might be something in you that was being satisfied and not their need? Knowing thoughts like this came with increasing frequency to Stella these days, mother of a daughter now on half-term holiday with her father before returning to the expensive school that kept Stella impoverished. Her child did not seem to miss her, or need her. Coffin might be her replacement, which he would probably resent.

Coffin nodded and walked out of the shop, to sit at one of Max's tables and enjoy the evening sun. He was tired, Stella was right there, tired and anxious. Things weren't going well in his command. He had inherited too many generals and too few soldiers of the line. It was always the same when a division was hastily cobbled together from those who had seen too many campaigns and not enough victories.

Stella got to the top of the queue to find Ted Lupus next to her negotiating for a bottle of brandy and some aspirins. Belatedly and thoughtfully, as if some food might not be a bad idea, he added some milk and a box of eggs.

'It's my wife,' he said apologetically. 'She's lying down with a black bandage over her eyes. She says her eyes are going bad on her. Nerves, really.'

'I know the feeling,' said Stella with sympathy. 'It's hunger with me. I always get hungry when I'm anxious.'

Clara came from the back of the shop with a bottle of aspirin. 'Mother says to have these and she's sorry Mrs Lupus is not well.'

'How is your mother, Clara?' said Stella. Max was wrapping a large slice of quiche for her, she would offer some to John Coffin, they might eat supper together.

'Better, thank you.' Clara's hair was tied back in two short plaits, giving her a cheerful, businesslike air. 'How is Billy?' No one had told her how he was, she was worried for her friend.

'Getting well,' said Stella, looking at Ted Lupus, who gave a confirmatory nod. 'Soon have him back again.' She did not know if this was so, but it seemed the thing to say.

'Close friend of yours, eh?' said Ted Lupus. 'Good thing. You could say where he was.'

'Oh yes, we talk everything over.' said Clara, blushing slightly. She met her father's eye, and departed rapidly for the back room.

Stella gathered together her purchases, added a bottle of red wine, and went outside.

Coffin rose from his seat without a word, and they walked back to St Luke's Mansions in companionable silence.

As they neared the church, Stella said: 'How are things?'

'Bad,' Coffin said. 'But I'll survive.' Then he added thoughtfully, 'I think.'

He helped her inside the front door. 'And you?'

'About the same.'

She got her keys out of her bag. 'Come and have supper with me? I've got some wine.'

'I'd like that.'

'You can open the bottle.'

Over the claret (Stella had bought a good bottle), she said: 'What do you think about incest?'

Coffin frowned. 'Professionally or personally?'

'As a motive for murder.'

'No.' The frown did not lift. He took his wine to the window and stood silent for a moment, looking out. 'I take it you mean in the context of our present baroque affair?'

'Yes.'

'And you're talking about our little pair of performers, Bridie and Will.'

'You know?'

He turned round. 'It had crossed my mind.'

'Can't beat you, can I?'

'Easily, Stella.' Just give your mind to it, he thought. 'But I've been in this business a long while. Almost all dark thoughts have crossed my mind in my time.'

'I don't suppose it's true,' said Stella, putting the quiche into the oven to warm and getting out the salad. 'The incest thing.'

'It very well could be, but I don't think I'm going to dig it up.'

'You amaze me sometimes.' Stella was startled. 'You sound exactly like Mimsie.'

'Ah, she's the one.' He drank some more wine. 'Tap all she knows, and we might have these murders solved.'

'Do you think you ever will?'

He shook his head. 'No.'

He thought the case might be lined up in the Black Museum with all its artefacts of murder as one other of the unsolved mysteries of his new command.

'Things do happen,' said Stella, putting a consoling hand on his.

THIRTEEN

ONE OF THE PERILS of his new position, as John Coffin had discovered, and was discovering again two days later (it always came to him with a fresh shock of surprise, he didn't feel like the John Coffin he knew), was the number of public dinners he was obliged to attend. The stern gaze of his secretary as she handed the invitations to him ensured he accepted far more than he would have wished. Once he got to the dinner, he often enjoyed himself, but he was always depressed as he got ready.

Tonight was the dinner of the New City Medico-Legal Society, at which he was due to speak.

Another cause for depression.

His evening suit needed brushing, someone's cat appeared to have moulted over it. Another cause for depression.

He brushed away at a deposit of white hairs. A bad case of mange here, he thought. Some hairs seemed to have a silvery tip, but all clung on to the jacket tenaciously.

He remembered now that after his last function he had given a lift home to the Senior Hospital Administrator of St Gervase's Hospital, and the fur was off her white fox cape.

His jacket was clean of fur, but some tufts of white had mysteriously managed to get on his trousers now. He decided not to bother.

He had, however, prepared his speech with some care and even rehearsed it in front of the bathroom mirror where the acoustics aided voice production. It suited his style to have practised more than once, he was by no means a spontaneous speaker, but he knew himself to be capable of making some sensible observations if he had enough time. He could even manage a few jokes, but he had to think about them beforehand. He was modestly pleased when he got a laugh.

There wouldn't be too many laughs today, he was talking on Crime in the Inner City area at a time when he had seven bodies of his own, as it were, to raise the murder statistics. The Press would certainly be there to ask questions if they got the chance, and he would have precious little he could say to them.

Not my investigation, but I have full confidence in my officers. Superintendent Paul Lane and Inspector Archie Young are in charge, that would be it and not enough.

There had been a report waiting for him when he got home. He had not yet had time to digest the contents but he could remember the sting in it.

Another blot on his evening was that his half-sister, Letty Bingham, was to be at the dinner. They were not on the best of terms just now. Between Letty and John Coffin stood the matter of his mother's diary, which she was threatening not to let him see. 'It's so private, John. I honestly think only another woman should read it.' And what she meant by that he was not quite sure, but whatever it was, he wasn't going to stand for it. Letty ought to know him better than that.

She was representing The Society of Professional Women, and as such would be seated not far from him, and thus would have plenty of opportunity to comment on the murders and doubtless also much to say. She appeared to regard them as an attack on her property and his Force as failing in their duty in protecting that property.

For an educated woman Letty could be very naïve, but he had noticed before that where money was concerned even the sophisticated became silly.

He wondered how much Letty had gambled on this enterprise, and how much she stood to lose if it went wrong.

He didn't want to sit across from Letty in the full splendour and glitter of her evening dress, probably wearing the topaz and diamond earrings (she said they were topaz, but he had more than a suspicion that they were 'fancy' yellow diamonds), and have her mutter about 'budget cuts'. Or rent rises? After all, he was a tenant.

He wondered what she would say if she knew what he knew.

THE IDENTITY OF the fourth woman has been provisionally established as Veronica Peasden, known professionally as Vonnie Vanden, a club singer and stripper, Archie Lane had written. 'We are trying to get in touch with next of kin to see if the handbag, watch and rings can be identified positively. This may present problems owing to the time span. Veronica Peasden has been on the missing Persons list for six years.'

She appeared to have been strangled with a ligature as with the other victims. A nylon stocking, possibly her own.

Veronica was the longest missing of all the women and therefore presumably the first to be killed.

Of that group.

Because the most menacing information came later in the report.

The papers of the report fluttered down from the table where he had placed them as he brushed his jacket. It began to sound like an ossary down there, he thought as he picked them up, a charnel house, a place in which bones are kept.

There were traces, so Archie Lane informed him, of more bones. The soil underneath the floor was being examined, and small bits of bone were turning up.

The age of the bones was not yet determined, but a preliminary glance had shown the pathologists that they were human and not animal as had been at first speculated.

Or hoped, Coffin thought, animal bones would have been so much more desirable. But no, they were human. Apparently, if you knew about bones you could tell at a glance.

Coffin finished dressing, and picked up the telephone. Inspector Young was on the point of going home, but he took the call.

'Is it possible that St Luke's was built on the site of an old burial ground?' Coffin asked. 'Is there anything in the local records?'

'We considered that, sir. But there's nothing in any old map or parish records to suggest it.'

'A plague burial pit?' suggested Coffin. 'Probably wouldn't be on any map.'

'Quite true, sir, and we've been talking to a local historian from the Poly. He doesn't know of anything, but is working on it.'

'Roman bones?' asked Coffin hopefully. 'Vikings, Anglo-Saxons?'

'The path man thinks they're not that old. Until we know the age of the bone traces we can't do much. They are just little bits of bones, sir. So that presents a difficulty. But there's something else. Something I didn't put in my report because I've only just heard myself.' There was an odd note in his voice which Coffin picked up.

'Well?'

'I only have a verbal report on this. But I trust Ludbrook who is doing the work on the bones. I guess he's right, unsavoury as it seems.'

One more disturbing, even sinister, suggestion had surfaced. The bones had been cooked. The flesh removed from them by heat. Probably boiled, Inspector Archie Young said, with detachment.

Coffin thought for a moment, then decided to ask. 'Any sign of teeth marks on the bones?'

A cannibal in the area was just what he needed.

'Ludbrook is working on that,' said Young, still keeping his voice cool.

It might be, thought Coffin, that in digging up the dead women, they had really discovered the remains of someone's larder.

THE THOUGHT WAS more than enough to put him off his dinner.

A new hotel called Armourers' Wharf had gone up on an old bit of dockland just south of the Tower of

London. There was an ancient creek on one side and the river on the other, so that if there was a flood then the basement and ground floor of Armourers' Wharf stood a good chance of going under deep water. This was not mentioned in the publicity since the new Thames Barrier at Greenwich ought to protect them.

Armourers' Wharf was smart and expensive, and much patronized by the new young rich, of which there seemed to be many. Coffin had been to several dinners there already. The interior decoration had been done by a talented Italian who knew all about the cool northern light from the river and how to harmonize it with expensive chintz and pale furniture. But in this banqueting room, used for formal functions, the furniture was solid and dark, framed in curtains of natural silk, backed by a wallpaper of an expensive deep red stripe upon crimson which looked well by artificial light.

A pity not to enjoy his meal, because the hotel prided itself on what it called 'good English cooking', which meant steak and kidney pie or a saddle of lamb with redcurrant jelly. No Brussels sprouts, no boiled cabbage, but leeks in cream sauce and small roast onions.

Coffin, who did or did not do his own cooking, enjoyed this side of it, although when having a speech to deliver, he wished it could be speech first and then food, but his appetite remained good for food as at Armourers' Wharf.

Judging by the expensive, eager, hungry young faces he saw all around him whenever he came here the Armourers' proprietors had judged their market rightly. It was the new cuisine, newer than 'nouveau' and more filling, and rightly, because of the extra comestibles, even more costly. People said Armourers' Wharf was the highest priced hostelry in London at the moment.

Across the table, Coffin watched his sister Letty being deliberately charming to the man sitting next to her, a junior member of the government. 'You're wasting your time,' Coffin wanted to say to her, 'this chap is not in the Cabinet, he has no real power. He is five years or so short of being worth your attention.' He was never sure how much his sister understood the realities of the English political system, where power rested, and who it was worth bothering with.

Letty saw her brother watching her and gave him a slight wink. 'Leave me alone,' she was saying. 'I know what I'm doing.'

As Coffin ate his salmon mousse he remembered the story that had come to him as a part of official police information: that this young man was sleeping with the wife of an exceedingly eminent cabinet minister, and might, therefore, have his own manner of manipulating events. Accordingly, Coffin looked at his sister with respect. She had a way of sniffing out those who might be useful to her. No yellow diamonds tonight, but what looked like some good pearls.

He turned to his neighbour, Dr Marcia Glidding, whose name he had read on the programme before him. 'I see you are the first speaker.'

'Yes, I introduce you.'

She was secretary of the Society, he had noted. For a few moments they exchanged the sociabilities of dinner companions engaged in summing each other up. Marcia Gliddings was a pretty, bright-eyed woman who looked younger than her distinguished career suggested she could be.

'And of course, I know about your career.' His secretary had provided him with a brief synopsis, and Archie Young had obligingly added his contribution. 'You got the Peabody Medal this year. Congratulations.'

'Yes, I was very happy about that. But I had a bit of luck.'

'You need luck,' agreed Coffin seriously, while knowing that luck alone would not do it.

The arrival of the crown of lamb with its attendant crest of bones was an unpleasant reminder of what had turned up in the crypt beneath where he lived.

He accepted his helping. Thank goodness it was not stewed lamb. He had heard the chef at Armourers' prided himself on his Lancashire Hotpot. At this moment he did not desire to see a stewed bone.

Letty leaned across the table. 'Aren't I lucky, John, sitting next to this lovely man? He has just promised to find me a sponsor for a play festival which Stella and Lily and I are going to launch. He's a great admirer of Lily Goldstone. And don't you think the lamb is just the tiniest bit tough?'

'No,' said John Coffin, chewing resolutely. 'It's the new way of cooking meat. You're supposed to like real meat.'

Letty laughed. Her pearls dangled forward, just missing the redcurrant jelly and skimming over the onions in white sauce.

'You are a sourpuss, John. Wait till you read Mother's diary. You're in for something.'

He would like to have said something sharp and effective then, but his neighbour turned to him. 'There's something I want to say, but it's by way of being business, so perhaps you would rather I left it?'

'Until after my speech.'

'They'll offer you some brandy then. I shall take that as a signal.' She smiled.

I like this girl, Coffin thought. And she couldn't be quite as young as she looked. He had always been attracted to bright, professional women. At that moment, Stella's stock took a sharp downward turn.

All through the rest of the meal and the speeches, including his own (which he delivered at a fair speed, then sat down with relief), he was wondering what Dr Glidding had to say.

She did not leave him long waiting, as the brandy came round and more coffee was offered, she turned from her other neighbour, a man recognized as a famous banker, and smiled again.

Coffin's neighbour on the other side was a fat and cheerful female writer on crime, from whom it took longer to disentangle himself, she had a fund of amusing anecdotes, one of which seemed to lead without pause into another. As she paused at the finale of a story about her pet tortoise which had gone missing, he turned swiftly to Marcia Glidding.

'Quick, before we get into the story about the squirrel who comes in through her cat flap together with a hedgehog.'

'Do you think she knows what terrible fleas they both have?'

'I'll tell her later,' said Coffin, giving his arm a scratch. 'What is it you were going to tell me?'

Dr Glidding took a spoonful of brown sugar and stirred it into her coffee before speaking. Coffin could hear a jolly voice beginning on a story about a dead cat in a parcel on his other side; he waited.

'Forensic scraps are the stuff of my work,' she began. 'Little bits of odds and ends. Sometimes I get results that help the investigating team, sometimes not. But I think they are always glad they consulted me and my colleagues. I hope so. Anyway, when I told Archie Young about the material fibres probably coming from a uniform, he seemed pleased.'

'It's going to be useful.'

'I always include the tiniest detail, might sometimes be a bit speculative but I feel it all helps. I hadn't done my full report when I spoke to Archie.'

'He's a friend of yours?'

'His wife is. We were at college together... I did some more work after talking to Archie, I had found traces of red flocklike material, mere specks, on the uniform fabric. I didn't mention those to Archie. Now I think they might be important.'

Could be, Coffin thought. Never can tell.

'So I ran a check on the materials sent to me from the other bodies found in the crypt. On two others, the woman identified as March and the girl, Rosie Ascot, I found similar specks. It's all in my report now, of course, as much as I could truthfully say.'

'Any idea of the origins of these bits?'

She shook her head. 'No, I hadn't then. But I carried it in my mind. Hoping ideas would come. But they were a flock of some sort, part cotton, part wool. And red, a deep red. Or had been once. There was staining from the surrounding earth and loss of colour, of course, but a residual colour remained.'

She gave her coffee another fierce stir so that the contents swung to and fro.

'And then I came here tonight, and saw that wallpaper.' She nodded to the elaborate paper. 'That's flock, on the paper. The bodies may have been in contact with a red flock paper.'

'You mean they were wrapped in wallpaper.'

'Covered, perhaps just covered. Or the killer could have been in contact with it and transferred bits to the victims. It happens.'

It was a truth universally accepted that the murderer always left something of himself behind on the scene to the crime while taking something of the victim's away with him. The trick was to match the bits.

'If you could identify the material, then you might have a lead to the killer.'

Some years separated the deaths of the two women. Could a roll of wallpaper survive so long?

'The trouble is,' he said, 'in cases of this sort, if we knew where to look for the wallpaper, we would probably know who we were looking for.' But she was right, every little scrap of information counted. 'Any ideas?' he ended hopefully.

'No.' She shook her head. 'Tell you if I had.'

'We've got a lot of choice.' A whole wide metropolis of choice.

'There's always someone you ought to look at closer,' she said.

The banker leaned forward and said something about the Sir John Soane Museum and the medical exhibits there, did she know it? Clearly he believed it was his turn again now. On his other side, Coffin felt a hand on his arm and heard a murmur start up about the white donkey at the bottom of her garden.

Across the table, Letty gave him one of her sardonic stares.

He wouldn't tell Dr Glidding about the cooked bones, it didn't seem quite the conversation for the dinner table.

WHEN HE GOT HOME, he telephoned Archie Young. It was late, but he chanced it. It was his turn to add new information in return for the news about the bones.

'You've heard about the bits of red material found on the clothes of two victims?'

'Got the report before me.'

Did he read them in bed, Coffin wondered, it was approaching midnight.

'Got any ideas on where they could have been wrapped in a red flock wallpaper shroud?'

'Is that Marcia's idea?'

'Yes.'

'I thought she'd have a word with you but I didn't know she'd come up with that.' His voice was polite, because of whom he was talking to. However nice the Old Man was, you never forgot his position, not if you valued your promotion, but he sounded mildly put out: he ought to have been told first.

'She'd only just thought of it.'

'Red flock sounds a bit old-fashioned. I think my grandma might have gone for it. I don't know who has a taste for it now. I might try Amelia Marr, I suppose. After all, there is a connection between her and March.'

'Good idea, do that in the morning.'

There were other things that Inspector Archie Young had to do next morning, but he would, of course, do that which the Commander suggested. First clearing it with Superintendent Paul Lane also, because Young was a prudent soul, who covered his position. The commander might go, politics were involved, but the Superintendent would be around for a long while yet.

Mrs Marr was cool when Inspector Young arrived. She made no pretence of not knowing who he was. It was her job to know that sort of thing, just as it was his to know about her.

He had debated how to bring up the subject of red flock wallpaper and had eventually got a sample of something like it from a local Do-It-Yourself Shop. The manager of the shop told him that genuine flocked paper was too expensive for him to market and was out of fashion anyway, but Young had found something he thought would do. It was red and white wallpaper, even if not striped.

'No, never used anything like that,' said Mrs Marr, barely giving it a glance. 'Terrible stuff. Wouldn't be seen dead with it.'

The wallpaper was a red and white floral pattern, he had to admit it was pretty awful.

'The paper in question may have been a red and white stripe,' said Young hopefully. He did not quite believe in the paper himself, but if the Old Man said to try, then try he must. 'Ever seen anything like it?'

'Not in this house. I never go for red. You can see that.' She waved a hand.

Young had to admit that lemon and silver and gold were the other end of the spectrum. 'Yeah,' he said with surprise. 'It looks good. Sophisticated.'

Mrs Marr laughed. She recognized a backhanded compliment when she heard one.

'How long have you been in this house?'

'Twenty years. And my aunt before me. I'm not stripping the walls for you.'

He had put his hand on the paper. 'Just looking.'

'There are other people in the world.'

'WHAT DID SHE SAY?' asked John Coffin. He had requested to be told as soon as possible. In fact, Young had found this meant the evening since the Commander had been inaccessible all day, walled up inside a series of meetings. He was at home just before Archie Young got through.

'She said to try someone else.'

'Yes.' Coffin was thoughtful. 'There is another house, isn't there?' And Rosie Ascot was the connection.

HILLINGTON CRESCENT was quiet in the evening sun. No. 3 was quietest of all. The garden shed where Rosie Ascot had been found was boarded up. The house had padlocks on both back and front doors. No uniformed constable stood at the gate, but a watchful eye was kept from a distance. Patrol cars had been routed to pass at intervals.

The garden itself had been thoroughly dug over and then been left. The weeds were already sprouting, encouraged by the warm, humid summer. The cat from next door had undisputed possession of it now, and paced it at intervals, guarding his territory. Tiddles was not the Tilers' cat and never had been. His nominal home was next door, which he visited but seldom, preferring his freedom. Tucked away in his memory was a picture of men digging, he would be on the lookout for them, but they represented no threat to his dominion. Not like that other one, who had shouted and thrown stones at a cat investigating the shed as was his right and catly duty. Nor the woman who had screamed.

Other things he had seen from a windowsill, taken in with a calm yellow gaze on which human violence did not register.

From the top of the shed, he watched the two policemen walk down the path to the front door and let themselves in. The inside of the house was theirs, let them do what they liked with it. He closed his eyes.

'There's that cat again,' said Archie Young. 'Wonder if he's homeless?' He had a kind heart. 'Perhaps I should get the RSPCA in.'

'Didn't look lost to me.' John Coffin was marching up the stairs, followed by DI Young who realized what a privileged position he was in, and what a splendid thing it was to have a patron (if that was what the Commander was being) but it presented problems. Chief Superintendent Lane, not to mention the rest of the investigating squad, might not take kindly to this expedition.

He was throwing open the doors to the rooms and staring inside. DI Young followed. Should he say that all the rooms had been thoroughly gone over? He decided not to.

Coffin paid little attention to the room with the big bed and dressing-table in it. The wallpaper was pale blue with small birds flying across it. By the look of it, some years had passed since it was put up. The curtains were pale blue with no birds, so no red flock there.

He passed on to the empty room, which was still empty but dustier than ever. A windowpane was broken through which dried leaves and dead flies had deposited themselves on the windowsill. The paper on the wall had long since faded from what might have been pink to a pale biscuit.

He opened the cupboards in both rooms, closing them again without comment. You couldn't tell what colour paper had decorated them since time and dirt had coloured them all grey.

'No red wallpaper.'

'Did you think there would be?' asked Lane. But he was too sensible to say it aloud.

Coffin moved on to the lumber room. 'This is more hopeful. Come on, give me a hand.'

The drawers of an old chest were dragged open, but apart from a pair of old socks and a dead blackbeetle or two, they were empty. Several old suitcases were full of ancient shoes, none matching. Archie Young closed a case, sneezing from the dust.

'People don't keep odd shoes, do they?'

'This lot did.' Coffin opened another case. 'Perhaps he was a shoe fetishist.' He was beginning to think that nothing would surprise him about the late Peter Tiler. 'This looks more hopeful.' The suitcase contained several old tins of paint, but nothing else. No rolls of wallpaper. 'Nothing there.' He stood back, brushing his hands on his trousers. 'Funny room, this. Smells, doesn't it?'

It did, but no worse than the rest of the house, Young considered. He didn't like the place, never had and never would now. Too much death around.

'I went over this place myself, sir, and I can't say I remember rolls of wallpaper anywhere.'

Various police searchers had examined the house at different times, all thoroughly according to their fashion. It still bore traces of their activity.

'Wild goose chase, eh? Well, you may be right.'

One of those intuitive ideas of his, thought Coffin, that were sometimes right and sometimes quite wrong. Lately, they seemed to have been more unhelpful than usual. Perhaps age had something to do with it. A declining faculty?

They stood in the kitchen. The evening sunlight came through the window over the sink. In the distance they could see the cat on the shed roof and he could see them.

The door to the lavatory where Mrs Tiler had been found hanging stood open.

Coffin went over and stood staring at the white painted wall. 'You know we haven't paid enough attention to Mrs Tiler. Her case is different.'

'She was strangled, sir. They were all strangled.'

'But not hung up as if to simulate suicide. And we don't know about Tiler himself,' Coffin reminded him. 'He may not have been strangled.' The pathologists were working on it, but death had probably come from a blow to the head.

'We are taking all that into account,' said Young stiffly.

'Yes, yes. I'm not blaming you.' Coffin turned back into the room. 'I haven't thought it through myself. We need to know more about Mrs Tiler.'

'There doesn't seem much to know, sir. She seems to have been almost non-existent as a person.'

'Mimsie Marker said more or less the same thing.' And had said that all the Tilers married such wives, or turned them into zombies.

'You can't believe all that old bag tells you,' said Young heartily.

'I like the old woman.'

'Oh, I do myself, we all do. But she can tell a tale. I heard she'd been taken ill with this bug that's going round. So I asked her how she was when I went to buy a paper.'

'She'd keep on her feet if she was dying.'

'I think she'd started the tale herself. Wanted a bit of sympathy. She'd had a fight with a neighbour and had a black eye.'

'What was the fight about?'

Young shrugged. 'Internecine war round here sometimes. Old quarrels, old scores.' He sounded amused.

Mimsie had said something like this, too. Look at family relationships, she'd said. As had his brother William. If anyone knew about family relationships, he ought to, if anyone did.

'You lived here long yourself, Young?' he asked. 'You seem to have got the hang of things.'

'No, came here about three years ago. But I'm interested in old habits and old ways. I like to find out. Also, I've found it pays to know your district in depth.'

Through the kitchen window they could both see the cat advancing across the garden towards them.

John Coffin turned towards Young whose face looked pink and rosy in the evening sunlight. Ought to let the lad get home to his wife, he thought. 'What about the shed?'

'That's completely empty now. We've had the whole floor dug up.'

'How's your wife?'

'Splendid, sir.' Young sounded surprised. 'She's writing an article for some American police journal.'

'On women and crime?'

'Oh no, that's not her speciality. On computer crime,' said Young in a respectful tone. 'She has an accountant's training too.'

The cat completed his journey with a leap to the windowsill, where he sat washing his face.

'Want to go on looking round, sir? We haven't done the ground floor.'

'No. There's nothing here.'

The cat completed one side of his face, then turned to start on the other, dabbing away without much plan. Clearly, his mind was not on the job.

'Not much of a washer, is he?' said Young.

'Better than we'd be without soap and water and laundries.' Suddenly he wondered how early hominids had washed. Had they licked their hairy limbs?

'I wonder if I ought to take him home. He does seem lost.'

Coffin turned away. 'Next time we come,' he said absently. 'Young, that lavatory where we found Mrs Tiler was once a washplace, so the WPC said.'

'That's right.' He followed Coffin in that direction.

'So it would probably have had somewhere to boil clothes. One of those old-fashioned coppers built into the wall with a fire underneath.'

'Might have had, sir.'

'See if you can find the builder who did the alteration. And when. Or anyone who knows anything about it. Get on to Ted Lupus. It's the sort of thing he'd know about. Also if there are any coppers like that still around.'

For the boiling of a body, such an apparatus might be quite the thing.

The house was locked behind them, safe against all intruders, except the fieldmice, who were permanently camped out behind the kitchen stove, and the cat, who had his own ways of getting in.

STELLA PINERO WAS standing by her own front door in St Luke's Mansions, her arms full of a huge bunch of lilies. She greeted John Coffin with pleasure.

'Aren't they funereal? From an American admirer. He must have just asked the florist to send the most expensive flowers they had. I love the smell, although I know one shouldn't.' She looked up at Coffin, her eyes glinting with amusement. 'Perhaps because of the address, they thought I *was* a funeral.'

'Would you like a cat? There seems to be one going spare.'

'No, I think not. Whose cat is it? You *do* look tired.'

'My sergeant thinks it is lost. Not quite sure if I agree with him.' He had taken her flowers while she got her key out. He knew very well that she still had uneasy feelings about entering her flat alone. 'Yes, I am tired.'

'What have you been doing? Let me give you dinner. I believe I have a casserole somewhere.' Stella looked around her as if the dish might be in the hall.

'Looking for some red flock wallpaper.'

Stella raised her eyebrows. 'For interior decorating? Which room? I thought Letty had done your place quite beautifully.' She had retrieved her flowers. 'I might take these flowers to Little Billy. I'm going to try to visit him . . . I don't quite see you with red flock wallpaper. Where on earth are you going to put it, even if you find it, which you might not these days, hasn't been fashionable for yonks, although I believe the young fogeys have taken it up.' Stella, when writing her own dialogue, never built in pauses for breath. 'But it's not you, John.'

'Police business.'

'Don't be pompous, my dear.'

He gave her best. 'Something like it may have been used to wrap or cover a couple of the murder victims. Bits of red embedded in the clothes. I don't suppose you've seen anything.'

'Come and have dinner and I'll think.'

He hesitated. 'I ought to ask you.'

'No, don't be silly, we don't play turns, I've got lots of food. I got it in for Charlie, we were going to discuss plans, but he's buggered off with some excuse about feeling seedy. Other fish to fry, I expect.'

'If you're sure . . .' But he knew he meant to accept. Stella was becoming a habit. Dr Marcia Glidding's stock dipped sharply, and Stella's went up.

'Oh, by the way, I've had a word with Bridie and Will, told them I know what was upsetting them and to treat it as rubbish. I think I've settled them down.

Good stuff in both of them, I don't want it ruined.'
There was something between a plea and a command
in her voice, a combination only an actress of skill
could produce.

'I don't think they killed anyone,' Coffin answered.

OVER DINNER, which was indeed a casserole, Stella
said: 'I can't do you red flock wallpaper, but I recall
some old red curtains that were around. Used to hang
at the church door when it was a church. I found a
rolled up bundle in the Theatre Workshop basement
when we moved in.

'What did you do with them?'

'They smelt horrid. Dust, dirt and goodness knows
what. I imagine what I would have done was to tell the
ASM to get rid of them.'

'And what would he or she have done?'

'A girl at the time, as I remember. I expect what she
did was to ask the caretaker to throw them out.'

Stella went out to bring in some cheese biscuits, she
had shopped for Brie, but with Coffin in mind (she
remembered what he liked), she also bought some
strong Cheddar.

As she came back, she said: 'About the cat, if it's
really starving, of course I'll have it.'

FOURTEEN

BY THE NEXT MORNING, the acting stage manager, a plump girl called Polly Lindsey, said she had asked the caretaker to remove the curtains and burn them, or take them to the nearest dump, and she supposed he had done that. She hadn't checked.

'They'd been around for ages. He seemed to know all about them. Almost as if they were his.'

'And that was Peter Tiler?'

'It was Tiler. He got the sack soon afterwards.'

DI Lane ordered a search of the nearest rubbish disposal tip, an order not well received by the three constables detailed to do it. But the men in charge of the rubbish showed a surprising willingness to help.

'It makes a change, mate,' said one of them. 'But don't count on finding anything. Too long ago.'

But after a muttered conversation between them, he vouchsafed that Ginger Griffin over there (Ginger nodded and smiled nervously) remembered a sack of red curtains which had been taken home by another man, a casual helper, now departed, who thought he could make use of them.

'What's the man's name? And where does he live?'

A little reluctance was shown by Ginger Griffin to pass on this information, but eventually he produced a name and what might be an address.

'Old Bean, we called him, and he had a caravan on a derelict site down by the Spinnergate station.'

After consultation with Inspector Young, a detective-constable was despatched to find Old Bean.

The caravan site was large and informal, with a shifting population. It was an opportunist collection of vehicles without any legal right to be there. The whole area would be cleared soon and a block of office put up. It did not look as if it was going to be easy to lay hands on Old Bean. He was said to have moved to another site.

'Go on looking,' ordered DI Lane. And when they did find him, then what? he thought cynically. Another lead that led nowhere?

But afterwards he was to think: No, the Commander was right. Not the red flock, curtains or wallpaper or whatever in themselves, but what came with them; it was the opening up point. It was what followed.

There is always such a point in a successful investigation and you never know when it will come. And as a rule, you only recognize it in retrospect. The canny and the clever know it when it comes. John Coffin looked to be one of that number.

And if you asked him how, he might not know. 'By the pricking of my thumbs,' he might answer.

Meanwhile, in another aspect of the case, the police pathologists were willing to advance the view that the small amount of bones scattered through the soil underneath the floor of the crypt made up one person. Or what was left of her.

For the body had been female. No head had been found, so they ventured on the speculation that this body might never be identified.

'Not unless we get a confession,' said Chief Superintendent Lane to DI Young. 'But I don't think this beggar, if we ever catch him, will be in the confessing game.'

The tentacles of the investigation were spreading out wider and wider.

Archie Lane remembered John Coffin's suggestion of talking to Ted Lupus about any improvements to the house in Hillington Crescent, but Ted had taken a flight from the new City Airport to Paris on business and was not available. Kath Lupus was at home, but she knew nothing. Ted's secretary, left in his office, said that her boss would be back on an evening flight, when she would tell him he was wanted.

An architect had confirmed that Yes, there were signs that there had been a boiler at one time in the ground-floor lavatory of Hillington Crescent. He was able to point to the marks where there had once been a chimney.

An old resident of the Crescent recalled the boilers, had had one herself but had replaced it with more modern equipment soon after the war.

'Then about ten years ago, it got fashionable to have an automatic washing machine in the kitchen and turn the washplace into a shower-room with a lav. A lot of people did that. There was a firm came round doing it.'

No, she didn't recall the name of the firm.

Ted Lupus, when contacted by Archie Lane himself, was more helpful. For Ted, it had been a normal working day, even the trip to Paris was nothing out of the way for him nowadays.

He came round to the police station in Spinnergate where the central office for this investigation had been established. Briefcase in hand, raincoat over his arm, he looked straight off the flight from Paris. 'I hear you are looking for me?'

'Good of you to come round, Mr Lupus.' Archie Lane, surprised while drinking a cup of coffee and typing a report, stood up, uneasily aware that he hadn't shaved well that morning and that his suit could do with a brush. Ted Lupus's suit had come from Jermyn Street and his tie from New York.

'Spoke to my secretary on the car 'phone as soon as I landed, and drove straight round. What is it? What can I do? Something about the boy? I thought he was mending.'

'I believe he is. No, it's just something we thought you could help with. An inquiry about the Tiler house in Hillington Crescent.'

'Get on with it then, I've had a tiring day.'

Archie Young was embarrassed. 'There was no real need for you to come here, sir, although I'm grateful to you for doing so. I wanted to call on your professional knowledge. Ask you about the lavatory in the Tiler house.'

'What about it?'

'It seems it might have had an old-fashioned boiler in it once. You know that sort, a copper to boil the clothes in and a fire underneath to heat the water.'

'I believe they did have. They were built just after World War One, a bit old-fashioned even for then.'

'We wondered when and how the Tiler house got rid of its boiler.'

'Not my firm.'

'I didn't think so, Mr Lupus, but we thought you might know which one.'

He shook his head. 'I don't know. I seem to remember a firm going round touting for that sort of business at one time. About ten years or so ago. A cowboy outfit. I think they've gone out of business. Is this really important?'

'Just might be. Or it might be on the periphery of the investigation. It's the date we're trying to establish.'

'Why do you want to know about the boiler? Or shouldn't I ask?'

'I'd rather not say just now. I dare say it will come out eventually.' It certainly would do, and cause a sensation.

'They were pretty big, those boilers,' said Ted Lupus. He had gone white. 'Women did a lot of washing those days. Do still, but they don't boil so much.' He put a hand against the wall to steady himself.

'Are you all right, sir?' Archie was concerned.

'Just a touch of the bug going round, I expect... I'm wondering what you think the boiler was used for.'

'I shouldn't dwell on it, sir.'

There was a moment of silence. Ted Lupus shrugged. 'Right. I'll get off home if I can't do any more. If I think of anything, I'll let you know.'

Archie Lane walked with him to the door. There was the car, a nice big BMW, nothing flashy, but sound and reliable and expensive. He watched the car drive away. The chap hadn't looked well. He passed his hand apprehensively over his own stomach. Surely he himself wasn't going down with the bug, too?

When he got home, Ted Lupus calmed his wife, who was distraught at his late arrival, and poured himself some whisky.

The murders were very much more horrible than he had supposed. He had not been impressed by his talk with Inspector Young. It seemed to him the police were getting nowhere.

'A drink, Kath?'

'Where have you been? The flight got in hours ago.'

'I had to go down to the police station. Would you like a nip, too?'

'What for?' She waved away a drink.

'Just some questions they wanted to ask. About a boiler, as a matter of fact. Can you beat that?' He gave a short, unamused laugh. 'Just don't dwell on it, that's my advice.'

He took a deep drink.

'The killings of those women were even worse than I'd imagined. And I thought I knew all about nastiness. Do you believe in cannibalism? Cooking up the dead and eating them? One way of disposing of the bodies. But the murderer had more coming in than he could eat.' Supposing he had said that aloud to her? He didn't, of course. But she could read something in his face.

'I think I will have a drink after all.' She got up to get one.

'Do you know, the police don't have any idea. Can't see their hand in front of their face. Someone ought to show them.'

'Don't drink too much, Ted.'

'Stupid clowns.'

'Don't you believe it,' said his wife. 'They get there in the end.'

They sat, drinks in hand, at their open window, looking at the River Thames which flowed, dark and silky, below them. Across the river were the lights of London. A light wind ruffled the water so that it glittered.

'What news of the boy? How is Billy?'

'I 'phoned Debbie. He's better, but not out of hospital yet.'

'Still silent?' asked Ted, who knew about the speaking problem.

'I don't know. I shall have a word with his mother. See what she says. I'm going to try to see him.'

'I wish you wouldn't. I think it took a lot out of you, that hunt for him. You've done your bit.'

Kath laughed. 'Half term is nearly over. I shall be back to doing my bit for about a thousand like him. I think I can manage Little Billy.'

'I'm sorry we haven't got any of our own.' He reached out to touch her hand.

'Not your fault, not mine. Anyway, I'm not trying to stand in as mother for Billy, don't think it, although he could do with one. Oh, by the way, I've had a call from someone calling herself an epidemiologist. They seem to be making a connection between my school, the epidemic and the party at the Black Museum. A focal point, she called it. That bloody Black Museum.'

'Take it easy, Kath, do.'

'Do you?'

No answer. She knew that neither of them took anything easily. That they had no children of their own had been their small quiet tragedy, but they had known other and bigger ones. Success in business, failure in business, love in the family, death in the family, they had known them all.

'That policeman, John Coffin, he's an outsider, he can't really know what this is all about,' she said. 'He'll get an answer, but he won't really understand.'

You needed to have lived around here all your life.

She did not say this aloud; it was the unstated but understood truth between them.

Ted Lupus believed it, Peter Tiler would have believed it, JoJo and Lily Goldstone half believed it, Will and Bridie had believed it, Charlie Driscoll still believed it. Mrs Marr was keeping an open mind, and Mimsie Marker believed she was the one who knew all.

All of them underestimated John Coffin's remarkable ability to draw disparate strands together and to make a whole picture of the deaths of Rosie Ascot, Amy March, Veronica Peasden and the others. In which list he did not forget the deaths of Peter Tiler and his wife.

And to see exactly the importance of the head and hands of Peter Tiler.

Synthesizing, it was called by scientists, and it went on deep inside him, emerging sometimes as a shout.

At the moment he had all the elements, could see a picture, but did not know why it had happened. That was soon to change. Shouting time was coming.

FIFTEEN

BUT THE FIRST SHOUT fell to old Tom Cowley of the Black Museum. Two days later, while DC Winter was still combing the caravan sites of London and its outskirts searching for Old Bean who lived in a trailer but liked to keep on the move and who might or might not have the red flock curtains, and while the bodies of all the women were being tidied and placed in neat, frigid drawers until the much adjourned inquest could take place, Tom shouted over the telephone. The head and hands of Peter Tiler had not yet been reunited with his body at this time, although it was about to happen, but Tom got his shout in first.

It was morning, breakfast-time, not Tom's breakfast-time, which was about six a.m., but John Coffin's breakfast-time which made it roughly two hours later. Still early indeed to be confronted with a bellow down the telephone.

'John, are you awake?'

'I am, Tom.' I am standing in my kitchen in St Luke's Mansions, holding my telephone in one hand and a cup of coffee in the other. The postman has just delivered my post with what looks like a parcel from my sister, Letty Bingham, and the gas bill. He put down the coffee cup.

'We've been broken into.' The outrage was strong. Coffin moved the telephone an inch or two further from his left ear.

'Where? Where are you speaking from, Tom?' Yes, the parcel was from Letty and it contained THE DIARY. He cradled the telephone under his chin and tried to get a look.

'The Black Museum, of course. We've been done over. You'd better get down here.' No thought of the rank of the man he was talking to, Tom was beyond caring about status, if he ever had.

Anything to shut Tom up while he got a look at his mother's diary. 'I'll look in on the way to the office.'

Within the hour he was with Tom in the Black Museum. Behind him lay an anguished telephone call to his sister Letty. He could not read his mother's writing. 'I can't make out a word!' Letty in return sounded both amused and calm. 'You have to get your eye in, John, I am surprised to have to tell a policeman that. Keep at it, a little at a time. Words will spring out at you and by degrees you will find you can read it. It will be worth it, I can promise.' He had thrown the diary to the ground in a fury, then picked it up tenderly to place it on his desk. Drat you, Mother, said an angry voice inside him, a puzzle to the end.

'Glad you're here,' said Tom. No words such as Thank you for the visit, or I know you are a busy man, passed his lips. 'Thought you weren't coming.' He was wearing a dark overall and carrying a brush and pan. 'We're a mess. It's a disgrace.'

The long low room which housed the museum was in an annexe to the Rainshill Police Station and thus around the corner from it and in the area which housed the garages for the patrol cars. It was easy enough to break into, perhaps a marvel it had never happened before, but now someone had done so.

Tables were overturned, chairs thrown aside and display cases broken into and their exhibits piled on the floor. Not destroyed, but heaped up, like jumble before it was sorted. There was broken glass from one display cabinet on the floor.

'You know what this is about, don't you?' said Tom. 'It's an attempt to close us down. They're at it, that's what they are.'

'Anything stolen?'

'No, not that I can see. But there wouldn't be.'

'Any idea who did it?'

Tom looked at him scornfully. 'If I knew I wouldn't be here, I'd be round nicking them.'

'How'd they get in?'

'Through the door, same as you and me. Double lock, but it couldn't keep out a bird.'

The lock had not been broken. The intruder had either had a key, or had known how to pick the lock. Neither was impossible. He or she (but surely the invader was male) had then, rather tidily now Coffin took another look, disembowelled the room. It looked contrived to him, not a real robbery at all.

'You know what it's all about? They want to close us down.'

Coffin didn't say Who does? because he knew he wouldn't get an answer from Tom in a state of paroxysm. Especially as he had yet another grievance.

'Something else as well. They're trying to blame the bug that's been going round on us. Did you know that? I had a woman doctor round here inquiring about that meal we put up for the visiting firemen. She says the kids at Madame Katherine Lupus's school started it. They had polio immunizations and the virus bred in their guts and they passed it on in full strength to people like you and me.' He made it sound a deliberate act of malice, not the simple working of a virus mechanism.

'Not quite blaming you,' observed Coffin mildly, moving around the room taking it all in. 'Who did the food?'

'Got the delicatessen chap, Max, to do it.'

'Goes back to him, then,' observed Coffin. Not good news for Max and the deli, if so.

On a table before him were laid out, as if for inspection, the rope from the display on Jim Cotton, the Leathergate strangler. Next to him, also laid out, were the exhibits from the rape and murder of two young women, a crime described by Tom, at that famous party, as one of their 'failures'. There were the stockings, the old raincoat and the sheet of yellowing newspaper with its faint, bloody fingerprint. It was the print of a thumb and across the ball of the thumb was a sickle-shaped scar. Coffin could just make it out.

'Don't you think it's odd, Tom, the way these objects are laid out? What do you think it means?'

'I dunno,' said Tom. 'You think about it.'

John Coffin absorbed his dismissal with the same good humour he had taken the initial summons. Old Tom was a law unto himself, and had to be accepted as such.

As he turned the corner into the main road, he got a glimpse of Stella Pinero striding towards the tube station bearing a large bunch of flowers. Not lilies, but roses. Roses for Little Billy?

STELLA WAS ALLOWED to see the boy, without realizing what an exception she was. Billy was up, dressed, and sitting at the end of the ward by the big television screen. It had proved impossible for him to keep up his act. Malingering was hard work. Urged forward by the doctors and positively prodded by the nurses, he had rejoined the world. Later today he was going home.

He accepted the flowers graciously, although fruit or better still chocolates would have been more welcome. He was glad to see that Stella had honoured him with a perfectly groomed appearance: a cream silk suit and a waft of Madame Rochas.

'You look better than I thought,' said Stella, giving him a hug. Ridiculous to be so fond of the little beast, but she was. It made her feel the want of her own daughter. 'We shall see you back at the theatre sooner than I thought.'

'My mother's taking me away for a holiday,' said Billy. 'Don't want to go but I've got no choice.'

'Where are you going?'

'Bermuda.' He tried to look as if the choice displeased him, but could not quite manage it.

'You lucky thing. We shall miss you.'

'I've had a bad time,' he said with some pride. 'I need building up.'

Stella put on a sympathetic face. 'Nasty virus. And then you were missing. We were all anxious. What did happen, Billy?' She tried to make the question sound casual, but he was not deceived.

Billy considered. He was aware that a cloud of scepticism hung over him. He needed to talk to someone and, in his experience of her, Stella had proved trustworthy.

'I hid because I thought the murderer was after me,' he said in a low voice. 'Still think so. Thought I was being followed. So I was, but not by the person I expected it to be. I hid there, but I saw the feet. Pretty shoes. With a nice heel. A lady's shoe.' He let that sink in, before saying: 'Wasn't Charlie, in case you were wondering. I know he dresses up. Helped him sometimes. I'd know his feet anywhere.'

Stella gave a small sigh, a mixture of relief and surprise. Thank God for a sophisticated theatre child, but he really knew too much. 'OK, not Charlie.'

'But I still think I was right to hide. I might have been killed.'

Stella looked at him. He was telling what he believed to be the truth. 'You can trust me. Something made you think you know who the killer was ... It's that pot, isn't it?'

He nodded. 'I was the one who found it in the gutter. Wish I'd left it there.'

Don't we all, thought Stella. But no, it was meant to be found. Someone would have picked it up.

Billy went on: 'Didn't mean anything to me at first, then I thought: I know where that came from and who could have used it.'

Stella said: 'I've had my thoughts too.'

That household that they had in common where pot plants flourished and such a bronzed urn as had encased Peter Tiler's head had been seen by both of them. She had seen a row of them on that terrace. Why had she not told John Coffin that final truth? Loyalty or a kind of fear about how it would touch the theatre?

'You going to say something? It's easier for you.'

'I'll see what I can do, Billy,' she said. 'Is there anything else you are worried about?'

'I shall be going away. I'll be safe. And I'm never going to say anything. You can count on that. I might do it when I'm grown up and safe. Only I guess you knew?' Stella nodded. She had had an idea for some time. One she had pushed aside because she could not see how it made sense with all those other bodies, but which nevertheless kept returning to her with irresistible conviction. 'But there's Clara in Max's. I talked to her.'

'But who would know you talked to Clara?'

'Mum does. And she might have said. I dare say she would have done. As things are.' The hint was clear.

So Clara might be in danger?

STELLA WALKED HOME. She needed the exercise and she wanted to think. The first thing to do, she decided, was to go into Max's where she might find Clara. It was still half term so Clara was safe as far as that went.

A soft rain began to fall from a heavy sky as she approached Max's. What did you say to a murderer if you happened to meet one: Good morning, and I know you are guilty? Or just keep quiet like Little Billy? Who could be wrong, she reminded herself. Still, there was a case to answer.

There was no personal risk to her, she told herself, but a precaution might be sensible. In her youth she had acted in more than one thriller where the heroine nearly gets killed when a sensible telephone call could have saved her.

Passing a callbox, she made a call to John Coffin. He was not there, but she left a message saying she was going to talk to Clara in the deli and it was important. Would he call her there?

This was the last anyone heard from Stella Pinero at this time.

JOHN COFFIN was not slow in getting back to his office, but Stella's message had been sitting there on the pad, awaiting his attention for something over an hour when he read it. There was other urgent business, an important call from Belfast about a terrorist who might be in his district, Celia had not thought what Stella had to say important.

When he read the message, Coffin decided to go straight to Max's himself.

Max, his mind full of his own worries about his food and the spread of infection, greeted him politely but seemed surprised. No, he did not know where Miss Pinero was. Lovely lady, he always enjoyed seeing her, serving her was an honour, such style she had.

And Clara? Again he looked surprised. No, she was not here either, she had received a call from her headmistress, Mrs Lupus, and had gone to meet her.

'Where?'

Max did not know. At the school, he imagined. Or possibly where Mrs Lupus lived. Such a nice lady, an honour for Clara to go to her.

'Can I use your telephone?' asked Coffin. Overriding questioning voices, he ordered inquiries to be made at the Theatre Workshop, the Lupus office and the Lupus home, and yes, the school. Yes, Stella Pinero and the girl Clara, please.

He put the telephone down, half believing that he would turn round to see Stella walk into the shop.

Max said: 'Mr Coffin, if I could talk to you, please, about the epidemic . . .'

'Later, Max.'

He walked out of the shop, not clear which way to go, but knowing he must find Stella.

The rain was coming down heavily now, shrouding the sky, while a wind gusted off the river, pushing strings of dark clouds across the sky.

He walked down the main road, leaving Max's deli behind him on his right. Ahead and to his left was the new Dockland railway, with the river beyond.

He could see on the skyline the profile of the big bleak school building where Kath Lupus presided. Nearer at hand was the block of flats, built into and around a former warehouse where Ted and Kath lived. There was an outer courtyard running down to the river's edge, together with an inner courtyard planted with geraniums. He walked towards this block.

Immediately facing him across the road was a row of garages. He could see something small and pale lying on the pavement.

When he got up to it, he saw it was a white handbag. One he had seen often before. As he picked it up a breath of scent came towards him. Stella's handbag.

A police car drew up at the kerb at that moment, a plain clothes detective and a woman detective with him.

'Go to the Lupus flat, I'm going for the river.'

He ran down the courtyard, turned on to the river walk where only a low wall offered protection from the long drop down to the water. The walk curved round the building and out of sight.

He started to run. As he ran he heard a scream. A loud scream from a throat that knew how to project sound. A theatrical scream. Stella's scream.

Even as he ran, he thought: Good for you, Stella, that's as much a shout as a scream.

A second later he heard the splash of water.

SIXTEEN

'THOUGHT THEY WAS ALL a goner,' said the old waterman, pipe still in his mouth, although he was soaking wet. 'When I saw them slip over the side, I thought: That's it, we've lost them.'

'Good job you were there.'

'Oh, I've seen plenty of men go in the water. You need to act fast. Accident, was it?' His eyes were bright and sceptical, he knew it was no accident.

'Yes,' said Coffin briefly.

'I heard the lady scream. Fair pair of lungs she's got.'

'Yes,' said Coffin again.

'Looked to me as if the older lady was pushing the girl and the other lady trying to drag her back,' said the waterman, his gaze brighter, his grin spreading more widely across his red weathered face. Not a lot of real humour in that grin, but a lot of cynical comprehension. He'd seen it all before on the river. 'Handy I was there fishing.' The River Thames produced a harvest of coarse fish, but this was his biggest yet.

'I'll get a police car to drive you home.' A note changed hands.

'No need, sir, I can row myself back.' He turned back to the steps leading down to where his boat was tied up. 'I hope the ladies will be all right. You're poisoned before you're drowned in the river, sir.'

Three ambulances were already leaving to take Clara, Kath Lupus and Stella Pinero to the hospital.

Coffin got to the hospital in time to find Stella vigorously protesting that she had not fallen in or been dragged in, but had jumped. 'I went in to save the girl. And I would have done, too, I've got my lifesaving medal. Only the old man in the boat pulled her out.'

She started on the story again, full of anger, more in shock than she knew. 'And I don't want to stay here, and I don't want that stuff, just some dry clothes,' she said to the nurse who seemed to be offering a sedative. 'I have a first night coming up.' She saw John Coffin. 'Oh good, you're here. Get me some clothes to go home in, please. Preferably my own.' She looked with disfavour at the hospital robe in which she was draped.

'Bless you, Stella,' said Coffin. 'Thank God, you are all right. They may just want to keep you here overnight to see.'

Stella visibly ground her teeth. Marvellous publicity, she reminded herself, but she did not intend to stay.

'Where is Clara?'

'Not far away. She's got her mother with her.'

'And Kath Lupus?'

Coffin shrugged. 'Just going to see.'

'She couldn't have killed all those women.'

'I don't know how you got yourself involved, Stella,' said Coffin, half loving, half exasperated. 'Except you always have to get into every performance.'

'I recognized where I'd seen that pot, that urn. So did Billy.'

Coffin groaned. 'You're two for a pair.' But he held her hand tightly and felt it gripped back.

A minute later he was looking down on Kath Lupus. She stared at him silently, but he wasn't sure if she saw him. Shock can take so many different forms.

And she was ill. A high fever, the ward sister informed him quietly.

'You didn't kill anyone, Mrs Lupus,' said Coffin quietly. 'But you certainly know who did. And you would have drowned yourself and the girl to save a murderer. Or one murderer.'

Kath Lupus stared, then closed her eyes. The infection bred within the guts of a group of children immunized with live polio vaccine, passed on to Clara's mother where it went 'wild' and contaminated the food she prepared for the Black Museum and thence spread outward, had at last caught up with Kath.

It was a symbol, Coffin felt, for a worse infection in his district. One which had been embedded in the population for years.

Nearly two decades ago a girl had been strangled, but her killer had never been caught, although he had left a fingerprint behind. They had tried an area check, with a house to house fingerprinting of all males, but the killer had not been found. One of their failures, Tom Cowley had said. A young policeman had been suspected of her death, but released without being totally cleared. Later, his wife having died in childbirth, he had killed himself.

The real killer, Coffin knew, had rested for a while, then taken up his labours again.

At the hospital entrance, Coffin met Archie Lane. 'Turn back,' Coffin said, 'and do what I tell you. Get a print of the hand of Peter Tiler, as delivered to us in the pot with his head, and see if the thumbprint matches the print on the newspaper in the Black Museum... I think that is why we were given the head and hand, to point out to us a long-unidentified killer. It was a revenge killing.'

'I've got Ted Lupus outside,' protested Archie Lane. 'He's come to see his wife.'

'I want a word with him,' said Coffin. He threaded his way through the crowds arriving for the hospital visiting hours. Across the taxis and buses he saw the BMW.

TED LUPUS WAS just getting out of his car. He stopped when he noticed Coffin. 'I've come to see Kath.'

'You'll see her later. And she'll see you.'

'She's ill. Not herself.'

'I know that as well as you do. Better, perhaps. Get back in the car. We can talk there.'

'Kath's done nothing.'

'She tried to protect you. But of course, in doing so, she accused you.'

Ted Lupus gripped the steering-wheel of the BMW. 'Shall I drive? Or do we just sit here.'

'Drive if you like, but don't try anything silly.'

'Not my style.'

No, silliness was not his style, thought Coffin. He was a practical man who had keys, to the St Luke's complex to move around in freely, into Stella's flat when he wanted, and into the Black Museum, too. He probably knew how to get into most of the buildings in the district.

'What about Peter Tiler, then?'

Ted Lupus drove out of the hospital, swinging left into the main road that ran parallel with the river. He did not argue, a pragmatist, he accepted what was coming. But he still wore his black armband, and that said something about him too.

'You have any idea why I killed him?'

'I think so. You certainly tried your best to tell us. You broke into the Black Museum and laid out the exhibits.'

'I thought you'd never get there. I wanted him dead once I realized he was the killer whose fingerprint was on that paper in the case. I saw it at that party in the Black Museum. And I'd seen his thumb times enough. Noticed it when I was working in St Luke's.'

'Why didn't you just tell us?'

'I wanted him dead. Not resting in prison, then coming out again after so-called life.' There was deep anger in his voice. 'And I wanted to do it myself. It was my job. But I also wanted him known for what he was.' A low rumble came out of his throat. 'A man who killed women.'

He drove on in silence. They were passing the Tube station where Mimsie Marker gave them a sharp look. Ted Lupus waved to her. 'There she is. You should have asked her. Bet she knows all about it.'

'You could be right.

'Mimsie knows that my young sister was the wife of the policeman who was accused of the strangling. My sister died. She died of grief and the kid with her.' Unconsciously, he glanced at the black armband. 'Her husband hanged himself. For years I could never make up my mind if he was guilty or not. Not until that day in the Black Museum. And then I thought: Peter Tiler, of course. We all knew the Tilers were a rotten lot. Even then I didn't know how rotten. Not till all the bodies turned up.'

'But you admit you killed him?'

Ted Lupus had driven back to his own home, taking the route automatically. The courtyard leading to the river walk was straight ahead.

Thoughtfully Ted said: 'After all, I might not have killed him. I cling to my life with the best.' He turned to give Coffin what might have been a smile in happier circumstances. 'This is just between you and me. I shall deny I said anything. Got that?'

'Go on,' said Coffin. 'I'm not promising. It takes two to play that game, and I'll get you if I can.'

Ted Lupus shrugged. 'I enjoy what I've got. I didn't want to throw it away, but when I went round to Hillington Crescent I couldn't get an answer. I went round the back and in through the garden door. I remember there was a cat on the window, looking in. And I saw that poor Tiler cow, hanging there. I think she must have threatened to go to the police. I knew Tiler had done it. He came in from the garden shed as I stood there. He looked at me. Just looked. He almost seemed to smile. Then I hit him. Couldn't stop myself. You'd have done the same yourself.'

'I might not have done the rest of what you did.'

'I have to say I enjoyed it. I put him in the back of the car. Yes, this one you're sitting in now. Took him to the yard and did what I did, then I hosed the place down. I kept the head overnight in the freezer in the empty flat. I got the pot from our place and the label I pinched next day from the funeral parlour. My firm was doing some work there. I needed the label to put an address on. I didn't want the head and the hand going to any old rubbish dump. I wanted you lot to see. And mighty slow you were. What was left of him I buried a bit later that night in St Luke's. Of course, I didn't know what company he had there. Kind of poetic justice, wasn't it?'

'You could say so.'

'Then I left the head in the urn in the yard at the theatre for anyone to find. There's quite a few of those urns around, you know. Plenty of other people round here have one, your sister included. Yes, that makes you wince, doesn't it?'

'Not really,' said Coffin, thinking that Ted would have a hard job involving Letty in anything.

'I am sorry I left his other hand and so on in ...'

'Teeth,' said Coffin. 'That was what you left with the head.' He really minded about those teeth because Stella had.

'I wanted him dead. It was really a good moment. I shouldn't say that, should I? But it was. Just as the worst was when Kath guessed.'

He drove the BMW into the courtyard. 'I usually park here ... I could drive straight ahead, over the parapet and into the river. Both of us. We couldn't get out. I've locked the car doors.'

'But you won't,' said Coffin, not touching him.

'No.' Ted Lupus started to back the car. 'I'm going to turn round, drive to the hospital, see my poor Kath, and then you can do what you like with me.'

As they neared the hospital, he said: 'That business with the boiler ... Did Peter Tiler eat flesh?'

'AND DID HE?' asked Mimsie Marker, who of course had heard everything and knew everything and needed to check this last item to add to her memories. She handed Coffin the evening paper where the case had brought big black headlines. The general belief in the neighbourhood was that Ted Lupus would plead guilty to manslaughter and would somehow get away with it. There was a long tradition of getting away with things in Coffin's new area of command. Then Ted and Kath might move away, go abroad, or they might stay here and face it out. That was in the tradition of the neighbourhood, too. Coffin would learn.

'No, I don't think so. No sign of teeth marks on the bones. Just a way of disposing of one of the bodies that Tiler tried and never tried again. I suppose they got rid of the boiler.' Perhaps his wife had guessed, poor woman, or tried to do a wash too soon. And there must have been a smell, you could never hide a smell.

'I always said to remember family relationships, didn't I?'

'You did, Mimsie.'

'Mind you, I didn't know what a kinky one he was for uniforms.' She sounded almost regretful at what she had missed.

So there was something that Mimsie did not know before me, thought Coffin.

'And how's Miss Pinero?' said Mimsie, giving her feline grin. Somehow she reminded Coffin of the black cat, who also knew the killer. Some weeks later, when the case was beginning to recede from the public mind, Stella sat alone in her flat. Behind her she had a very successful first night for her production of *Hedda Gabler* which had won high praise from all the critics. She was pleased, Letty Bingham was pleased, but now Stella was suffering from the reaction. A grey depression settled on her soul.

Is this all I've got to look forward to? she thought. A life alone in this place? Don't I want something more?

In low spirits, she went to her refrigerator (a new one) to get out a bottle of champagne. You could always pretend to be happy.

Then she heard her doorbell ring.

IN HIS SITTING-ROOM at the top of the tower, Coffin had been trying to read his mother's diary. He would look at a page until a word stood out, then he would throw the book some distance, pick it up, and try again. Occasionally, he would walk about the room, then come back to stare at a page in hope of illumination.

'Luck?' he said. 'Is that word luck?'

Or was it fuck? Surely not, Mother, he thought, shocked. But was that what Letty had meant? Was he in for a bath in erotica?

He felt a tap at his ankle and looked down.

'Right,' he said. 'I feel the need for a bit of company, too.'

When Letty opened her door, he was standing there with Tiddles under his arm. Somehow, neither cat nor man were sure how, they ended up together. Was it a life partnership?

'Can we both come in?'

LATER STILL than all this, Old Bean finally decided to settle for the winter in his favourite spot on the Essex coast. He knew the farmer who let him rent a bit of scrub land from which there was a fine view of the sea.

He unpacked his possessions with the idea of seeing what he could sell. He was a bit of a magpie, hoarding treasures both little and big, but occasionally they had to be turned into cash. A man must eat, and even more drink.

He shook out a roll of several old red curtains. What a stink, he thought. Wonder how many dead bodies have been rolled up in here? He smelt himself by the end of the summer and no bath, but you never know your own smell.

He folded the curtains up again, pushing them under his bed. He was a drinking pal of a man who bought old rags by weight, and they certainly weighed.

That night a great wind swept in from the Atlantic, bringing devastation to Southern England. Essex was in the front of the storm.

A huge oak tree fell across Old Bean in his caravan, crushing him and his bed into the red flock curtains on which he lay. Once again they were a shroud.